T0145497

When William Came

When William Came

Saki

MINT EDITIONS

When William Came was first published in 1914.

This edition published by Mint Editions 2021.

ISBN 9781513282909 | E-ISBN 9781513287928

Published by Mint Editions®

 MINT
EDITIONS

minteditionbooks.com

Publishing Director: Jennifer Newens
Design & Production: Rachel Lopez Metzger
Project Manager: Micaela Clark
Typesetting: Westchester Publishing Services

Contents

I. The Singing-Bird and the Barometer   7

II. The Homecoming   15

III. "The Metskie Tsar"   19

IV. "Es Ist Verboten"   28

V. L'Art D'Etre Cousine   35

VI. Herr von Kwarl   40

VII. The Lure   47

VIII. The First-Night   53

IX. An Evening "To Be Remembered"   61

X. Some Reflections and a "Te Deum"   68

XI. The Tea Shop   74

XII. The Travelling Companions   83

XIII. Torywood   89

XIV. "A Perfectly Glorious Afternoon"   96

XV. The Intelligent Anticipator of Wants   105

XVI. Sunrise   111

XVII. The Event of the Season   115

XVIII. THE DEAD WHO DO NOT UNDERSTAND   119

XIX. THE LITTLE FOXES   126

I

The Singing-Bird and the Barometer

Cicely Yeovil sat in a low swing chair, alternately looking at herself in a mirror and at the other occupant of the room in the flesh. Both prospects gave her undisguised satisfaction. Without being vain she was duly appreciative of good looks, whether in herself or in another, and the reflection that she saw in the mirror, and the young man whom she saw seated at the piano, would have come with credit out of a more severely critical inspection. Probably she looked longer and with greater appreciation at the piano player than at her own image; her good looks were an inherited possession, that had been with her more or less all her life, while Ronnie Storre was a comparatively new acquisition, discovered and achieved, so to speak, by her own enterprise, selected by her own good taste. Fate had given her adorable eyelashes and an excellent profile. Ronnie was an indulgence she had bestowed on herself.

Cicely had long ago planned out for herself a complete philosophy of life, and had resolutely set to work to carry her philosophy into practice. "When love is over how little of love even the lover understands," she quoted to herself from one of her favourite poets, and transposed the saying into "While life is with us how little of life even the materialist understands." Most people that she knew took endless pains and precautions to preserve and prolong their lives and keep their powers of enjoyment unimpaired; few, very few, seemed to make any intelligent effort at understanding what they really wanted in the way of enjoying their lives, or to ascertain what were the best means for satisfying those wants. Fewer still bent their whole energies to the one paramount aim of getting what they wanted in the fullest possible measure. Her scheme of life was not a wholly selfish one; no one could understand what she wanted as well as she did herself, therefore she felt that she was the best person to pursue her own ends and cater for her own wants. To have others thinking and acting for one merely meant that one had to be perpetually grateful for a lot of well-meant and usually unsatisfactory services. It was like the case of a rich man giving a community a free library, when probably the community only wanted free fishing or reduced tram-fares.

Cicely studied her own whims and wishes, experimented in the best method of carrying them into effect, compared the accumulated results of her experiments, and gradually arrived at a very clear idea of what she wanted in life, and how best to achieve it. She was not by disposition a self-centred soul, therefore she did not make the mistake of supposing that one can live successfully and gracefully in a crowded world without taking due notice of the other human elements around one. She was instinctively far more thoughtful for others than many a person who is genuinely but unseeingly addicted to unselfishness.

Also she kept in her armoury the weapon which can be so mightily effective if used sparingly by a really sincere individual—the knowledge of when to be a humbug. Ambition entered to a certain extent into her life, and governed it perhaps rather more than she knew. She desired to escape from the doom of being a nonentity, but the escape would have to be effected in her own way and in her own time; to be governed by ambition was only a shade or two better than being governed by convention.

The drawing-room in which she and Ronnie were sitting was of such proportions that one hardly knew whether it was intended to be one room or several, and it had the merit of being moderately cool at two o'clock on a particularly hot July afternoon. In the coolest of its many alcoves servants had noiselessly set out an improvised luncheon table: a tempting array of caviare, crab and mushroom salads, cold asparagus, slender hock bottles and high-stemmed wine goblets peeped out from amid a setting of Charlotte Klemm roses.

Cicely rose from her seat and went over to the piano.

"Come," she said, touching the young man lightly with a finger-tip on the top of his very sleek, copper-hued head, "we're going to have picnic-lunch today up here; it's so much cooler than any of the downstairs rooms, and we shan't be bothered with the servants trotting in and out all the time. Rather a good idea of mine, wasn't it?"

Ronnie, after looking anxiously to see that the word "picnic" did not portend tongue sandwiches and biscuits, gave the idea his blessing.

"What is young Storre's profession?" some one had once asked concerning him.

"He has a great many friends who have independent incomes," had been the answer.

The meal was begun in an appreciative silence; a picnic in which three kinds of red pepper were available for the caviare demanded a certain amount of respectful attention.

"My heart ought to be like a singing-bird today, I suppose," said Cicely presently.

"Because your good man is coming home?" asked Ronnie.

Cicely nodded.

"He's expected some time this afternoon, though I'm rather vague as to which train he arrives by. Rather a stifling day for railway travelling."

"And is your heart doing the singing-bird business?" asked Ronnie.

"That depends," said Cicely, "if I may choose the bird. A missel-thrush would do, perhaps; it sings loudest in stormy weather, I believe."

Ronnie disposed of two or three stems of asparagus before making any comment on this remark.

"Is there going to be stormy weather?" he asked.

"The domestic barometer is set rather that way," said Cicely. "You see, Murrey has been away for ever so long, and, of course, there will be lots of things he won't be used to, and I'm afraid matters may be rather strained and uncomfortable for a time."

"Do you mean that he will object to me?" asked Ronnie.

"Not in the least," said Cicely, "he's quite broad-minded on most subjects, and he realises that this is an age in which sensible people know thoroughly well what they want, and are determined to get what they want. It pleases me to see a lot of you, and to spoil you and pay you extravagant compliments about your good looks and your music, and to imagine at times that I'm in danger of getting fond of you; I don't see any harm in it, and I don't suppose Murrey will either—in fact, I shouldn't be surprised if he takes rather a liking to you. No, it's the general situation that will trouble and exasperate him; he's not had time to get accustomed to the fait accompli like we have. It will break on him with horrible suddenness."

"He was somewhere in Russia when the war broke out, wasn't he?" said Ronnie.

"Somewhere in the wilds of Eastern Siberia, shooting and bird collecting, miles away from a railway or telegraph line, and it was all over before he knew anything about it; it didn't last very long, when you come to think of it. He was due home somewhere about that time, and when the weeks slipped by without my hearing from him, I quite thought he'd been captured in the Baltic or somewhere on the way back. It turned out that he was down with marsh fever in some out-of-the-way spot, and everything was over and finished with before he got back to civilisation and newspapers."

"It must have been a bit of a shock," said Ronnie, busy with a well-devised salad; "still, I don't see why there should be domestic storms when he comes back. You are hardly responsible for the catastrophe that has happened."

"No," said Cicely, "but he'll come back naturally feeling sore and savage with everything he sees around him, and he won't realise just at once that we've been through all that ourselves, and have reached the stage of sullen acquiescence in what can't be helped. He won't understand, for instance, how we can be enthusiastic and excited over Gorla Mustelford's debut, and things of that sort; he'll think we are a set of callous revellers, fiddling while Rome is burning."

"In this case," said Ronnie, "Rome isn't burning, it's burnt. All that remains to be done is to rebuild it—when possible."

"Exactly, and he'll say we're not doing much towards helping at that."

"But," protested Ronnie, "the whole thing has only just happened; 'Rome wasn't built in a day,' and we can't rebuild our Rome in a day."

"I know," said Cicely, "but so many of our friends, and especially Murrey's friends, have taken the thing in a tragical fashion, and cleared off to the Colonies, or shut themselves up in their country houses, as though there was a sort of moral leprosy infecting London."

"I don't see what good that does," said Ronnie.

"It doesn't do any good, but it's what a lot of them have done because they felt like doing it, and Murrey will feel like doing it too. That is where I foresee trouble and disagreement."

Ronnie shrugged his shoulders.

"I would take things tragically if I saw the good of it," he said; "as matters stand it's too late in the day and too early to be anything but philosophical about what one can't help. For the present we've just got to make the best of things. Besides, you can't very well turn down Gorla at the last moment."

"I'm not going to turn down Gorla, or anybody," said Cicely with decision. "I think it would be silly, and silliness doesn't appeal to me. That is why I foresee storms on the domestic horizon. After all, Gorla has her career to think of. Do you know," she added, with a change of tone, "I rather wish you would fall in love with Gorla; it would make me horribly jealous, and a little jealousy is such a good tonic for any woman who knows how to dress well. Also, Ronnie, it would prove that you are capable of falling in love with some one, of which I've grave doubts up to the present."

"Love is one of the few things in which the make-believe is superior to the genuine," said Ronnie, "it lasts longer, and you get more fun out of it, and it's easier to replace when you've done with it."

"Still, it's rather like playing with coloured paper instead of playing with fire," objected Cicely.

A footman came round the corner with the trained silence that tactfully contrives to make itself felt.

"Mr. Luton to see you, Madam," he announced, "shall I say you are in?"

"Mr. Luton? Oh, yes," said Cicely, "he'll probably have something to tell us about Gorla's concert," she added, turning to Ronnie.

Tony Luton was a young man who had sprung from the people, and had taken care that there should be no recoil. He was scarcely twenty years of age, but a tightly packed chronicle of vicissitudes lay behind his sprightly insouciant appearance. Since his fifteenth year he had lived, Heaven knew how, getting sometimes a minor engagement at some minor music-hall, sometimes a temporary job as secretary-valet-companion to a roving invalid, dining now and then on plovers' eggs and asparagus at one of the smarter West End restaurants, at other times devouring a kipper or a sausage in some stuffy Edgware Road eating-house; always seemingly amused by life, and always amusing. It is possible that somewhere in such heart as he possessed there lurked a rankling bitterness against the hard things of life, or a scrap of gratitude towards the one or two friends who had helped him disinterestedly, but his most intimate associates could not have guessed at the existence of such feelings. Tony Luton was just a merry-eyed dancing faun, whom Fate had surrounded with streets instead of woods, and it would have been in the highest degree inartistic to have sounded him for a heart or a heartache.

The dancing of the faun took one day a livelier and more assured turn, the joyousness became more real, and the worst of the vicissitudes seemed suddenly over. A musical friend, gifted with mediocre but marketable abilities, supplied Tony with a song, for which he obtained a trial performance at an East End hall. Dressed as a jockey, for no particular reason except that the costume suited him, he sang, "They quaff the gay bubbly in Eccleston Square" to an appreciative audience, which included the manager of a famous West End theatre of varieties. Tony and his song won the managerial favour, and were immediately transplanted to the West End house, where they scored a success of which the drooping music-hall industry was at the moment badly in need.

It was just after the great catastrophe, and men of the London world were in no humour to think; they had witnessed the inconceivable befall them, they had nothing but political ruin to stare at, and they were anxious to look the other way. The words of Tony's song were more or less meaningless, though he sang them remarkably well, but the tune, with its air of slyness and furtive joyousness, appealed in some unaccountable manner to people who were furtively unhappy, and who were trying to appear stoically cheerful.

"What must be, must be," and "It's a poor heart that never rejoices," were the popular expressions of the London public at that moment, and the men who had to cater for that public were thankful when they were able to stumble across anything that fitted in with the prevailing mood. For the first time in his life Tony Luton discovered that agents and managers were a leisured class, and that office boys had manners.

He entered Cicely's drawing-room with the air of one to whom assurance of manner has become a sheathed weapon, a court accessory rather than a trade implement. He was more quietly dressed than the usual run of music-hall successes; he had looked critically at life from too many angles not to know that though clothes cannot make a man they can certainly damn him.

"Thank you, I have lunched already," he said in answer to a question from Cicely. "Thank you," he said again in a cheerful affirmative, as the question of hock in a tall ice-cold goblet was propounded to him.

"I've come to tell you the latest about the Gorla Mustelford evening," he continued. "Old Laurent is putting his back into it, and it's really going to be rather a big affair. She's going to out-Russian the Russians. Of course, she hasn't their technique nor a tenth of their training, but she's having tons of advertisement. The name Gorla is almost an advertisement in itself, and then there's the fact that she's the daughter of a peer."

"She has temperament," said Cicely, with the decision of one who makes a vague statement in a good cause.

"So Laurent says," observed Tony. "He discovers temperament in every one that he intends to boom. He told me that I had temperament to the finger-tips, and I was too polite to contradict him. But I haven't told you the really important thing about the Mustelford debut. It is a profound secret, more or less, so you must promise not to breathe a word about it till half-past four, when it will appear in all the six o'clock newspapers."

Tony paused for dramatic effect, while he drained his goblet, and then made his announcement.

"Majesty is going to be present. Informally and unofficially, but still present in the flesh. A sort of casual dropping in, carefully heralded by unconfirmed rumour a week ahead."

"Heavens!" exclaimed Cicely, in genuine excitement, "what a bold stroke. Lady Shalem has worked that, I bet. I suppose it will go down all right."

"Trust Laurent to see to that," said Tony, "he knows how to fill his house with the right sort of people, and he's not the one to risk a fiasco. He knows what he's about. I tell you, it's going to be a big evening."

"I say!" exclaimed Ronnie suddenly, "give a supper party here for Gorla on the night, and ask the Shalem woman and all her crowd. It will be awful fun."

Cicely caught at the suggestion with some enthusiasm. She did not particularly care for Lady Shalem, but she thought it would be just as well to care for her as far as outward appearances went.

Grace, Lady Shalem, was a woman who had blossomed into sudden importance by constituting herself a sort of foster-mother to the fait accompli. At a moment when London was denuded of most of its aforetime social leaders she had seen her opportunity, and made the most of it. She had not contented herself with bowing to the inevitable, she had stretched out her hand to it, and forced herself to smile graciously at it, and her polite attentions had been reciprocated. Lady Shalem, without being a beauty or a wit, or a grand lady in the traditional sense of the word, was in a fair way to becoming a power in the land; others, more capable and with stronger claims to social recognition, would doubtless overshadow her and displace her in due course, but for the moment she was a person whose good graces counted for something, and Cicely was quite alive to the advantage of being in those good graces.

"It would be rather fun," she said, running over in her mind the possibilities of the suggested supper-party.

"It would be jolly useful," put in Ronnie eagerly; "you could get all sorts of interesting people together, and it would be an excellent advertisement for Gorla."

Ronnie approved of supper-parties on principle, but he was also thinking of the advantage which might accrue to the drawing-room concert which Cicely had projected (with himself as the chief performer), if he could be brought into contact with a wider circle of music patrons.

"I know it would be useful," said Cicely, "it would be almost historical; there's no knowing who might not come to it—and things are dreadfully slack in the entertaining line just now."

The ambitious note in her character was making itself felt at that moment.

"Let's go down to the library, and work out a list of people to invite," said Ronnie.

A servant entered the room and made a brief announcement.

"Mr. Yeovil has arrived, madam."

"Bother," said Ronnie sulkily. "Now you'll cool off about that supper party, and turn down Gorla and the rest of us."

It was certainly true that the supper already seemed a more difficult proposition in Cicely's eyes than it had a moment or two ago.

> "'You'll not forget my only daughter,
> E'en though Saphia has crossed the sea,'"

quoted Tony, with mocking laughter in his voice and eyes.

Cicely went down to greet her husband. She felt that she was probably very glad that he was home once more; she was angry with herself for not feeling greater certainty on the point. Even the well-beloved, however, can select the wrong moment for return. If Cicely Yeovil's heart was like a singing-bird, it was of a kind that has frequent lapses into silence.

II

The Homecoming

Murrey Yeovil got out of the boat-train at Victoria Station, and stood waiting, in an attitude something between listlessness and impatience, while a porter dragged his light travelling kit out of the railway carriage and went in search of his heavier baggage with a hand-truck. Yeovil was a grey-faced young man, with restless eyes, and a rather wistful mouth, and an air of lassitude that was evidently only a temporary characteristic. The hot dusty station, with its blended crowds of dawdling and scurrying people, its little streams of suburban passengers pouring out every now and then from this or that platform, like ants swarming across a garden path, made a wearisome climax to what had been a rather wearisome journey. Yeovil glanced quickly, almost furtively, around him in all directions, with the air of a man who is constrained by morbid curiosity to look for things that he would rather not see. The announcements placed in German alternatively with English over the booking office, left-luggage office, refreshment buffets, and so forth, the crowned eagle and monogram displayed on the post boxes, caught his eye in quick succession.

He turned to help the porter to shepherd his belongings on to the truck, and followed him to the outer yard of the station, where a string of taxi-cabs was being slowly absorbed by an outpouring crowd of travellers.

Portmanteaux, wraps, and a trunk or two, much be-labelled and travel-worn, were stowed into a taxi, and Yeovil turned to give the direction to the driver.

"Twenty-eight, Berkshire Street."

"Berkschirestrasse, acht-und-zwanzig," echoed the man, a bulky spectacled individual of unmistakable Teuton type.

"Twenty-eight, Berkshire Street," repeated Yeovil, and got into the cab, leaving the driver to re-translate the direction into his own language.

A succession of cabs leaving the station blocked the roadway for a moment or two, and Yeovil had leisure to observe the fact that Viktoria Strasse was lettered side by side with the familiar English name of the street. A notice directing the public to the neighbouring swimming baths was also written up in both languages. London had become a bi-lingual city, even as Warsaw.

The cab threaded its way swiftly along Buckingham Palace Road towards the Mall. As they passed the long front of the Palace the traveller turned his head resolutely away, that he might not see the alien uniforms at the gates and the eagle standard flapping in the sunlight. The taxi driver, who seemed to have combative instincts, slowed down as he was turning into the Mall, and pointed to the white pile of memorial statuary in front of the palace gates.

"Grossmutter Denkmal, yes," he announced, and resumed his journey.

Arrived at his destination, Yeovil stood on the steps of his house and pressed the bell with an odd sense of forlornness, as though he were a stranger drifting from nowhere into a land that had no cognisance of him; a moment later he was standing in his own hall, the object of respectful solicitude and attention. Sprucely garbed and groomed lackeys busied themselves with his battered travel-soiled baggage; the door closed on the guttural-voiced taxi driver, and the glaring July sunshine. The wearisome journey was over.

"Poor dear, how dreadfully pulled-down you look," said Cicely, when the first greetings had been exchanged.

"It's been a slow business, getting well," said Yeovil. "I'm only three-quarter way there yet."

He looked at his reflection in a mirror and laughed ruefully.

"You should have seen what I looked like five or six weeks ago," he added.

"You ought to have let me come out and nurse you," said Cicely; "you know I wanted to."

"Oh, they nursed me well enough," said Yeovil, "and it would have been a shame dragging you out there; a small Finnish health resort, out of the season, is not a very amusing place, and it would have been worse for any one who didn't talk Russian."

"You must have been buried alive there," said Cicely, with commiseration in her voice.

"I wanted to be buried alive," said Yeovil. "The news from the outer world was not of a kind that helped a despondent invalid towards convalescence. They spoke to me as little as possible about what was happening, and I was grateful for your letters because they also told me very little. When one is abroad, among foreigners, one's country's misfortunes cause one an acuter, more personal distress, than they would at home even."

"Well, you are at home now, anyway," said Cicely, "and you can jog along the road to complete recovery at your own pace. A little quiet shooting this autumn and a little hunting, just enough to keep you fit and not to overtire you; you mustn't overtax your strength."

"I'm getting my strength back all right," said Yeovil. "This journey hasn't tired me half as much as one might have expected. It's the awful drag of listlessness, mental and physical, that is the worst after-effect of these marsh fevers; they drain the energy out of you in bucketfuls, and it trickles back again in teaspoonfuls. And just now untiring energy is what I shall need, even more than strength; I don't want to degenerate into a slacker."

"Look here, Murrey," said Cicely, "after we've had dinner together tonight, I'm going to do a seemingly unwifely thing. I'm going to go out and leave you alone with an old friend. Doctor Holham is coming in to drink coffee and smoke with you. I arranged this because I knew it was what you would like. Men can talk these things over best by themselves, and Holham can tell you everything that happened—since you went away. It will be a dreary story, I'm afraid, but you will want to hear it all. It was a nightmare time, but now one sees it in a calmer perspective."

"I feel in a nightmare still," said Yeovil.

"We all felt like that," said Cicely, rather with the air of an elder person who tells a child that it will understand things better when it grows up; "time is always something of a narcotic you know. Things seem absolutely unbearable, and then bit by bit we find out that we are bearing them. And now, dear, I'll fill up your notification paper and leave you to superintend your unpacking. Robert will give you any help you want."

"What is the notification paper?" asked Yeovil.

"Oh, a stupid form to be filled up when any one arrives, to say where they come from, and their business and nationality and religion, and all that sort of thing. We're rather more bureaucratic than we used to be, you know."

Yeovil said nothing, but into the sallow greyness of his face there crept a dark flush, that faded presently and left his colour more grey and bloodless than before.

The journey seemed suddenly to have recommenced; he was under his own roof, his servants were waiting on him, his familiar possessions were in evidence around him, but the sense of being at home had vanished. It was as though he had arrived at some wayside hotel, and been asked to register his name and status and destination. Other things of disgust and irritation he had foreseen in the London he was coming to—the alterations on stamps and coinage, the intrusive Teuton element, the alien uniforms cropping up everywhere, the new orientation of social life; such things he was prepared for, but this personal evidence of his subject state came on him unawares, at a moment when he had, so to speak, laid his armour aside. Cicely spoke lightly of the hateful formality that had been forced on them; would he, too, come to regard things in the same acquiescent spirit?

III

"The Metskie Tsar"

I was in the early stages of my fever when I got the first inkling of what was going on," said Yeovil to the doctor, as they sat over their coffee in a recess of the big smoking-room; "just able to potter about a bit in the daytime, fighting against depression and inertia, feverish as evening came on, and delirious in the night. My game tracker and my attendant were both Buriats, and spoke very little Russian, and that was the only language we had in common to converse in. In matters concerning food and sport we soon got to understand each other, but on other subjects we were not easily able to exchange ideas. One day my tracker had been to a distant trading-store to get some things of which we were in need; the store was eighty miles from the nearest point of railroad, eighty miles of terribly bad roads, but it was in its way a centre and transmitter of news from the outside world. The tracker brought back with him vague tidings of a conflict of some sort between the 'Metskie Tsar' and the 'Angliskie Tsar,' and kept repeating the Russian word for defeat. The 'Angliskie Tsar' I recognised, of course, as the King of England, but my brain was too sick and dull to read any further meaning into the man's reiterated gabble. I grew so ill just then that I had to give up the struggle against fever, and make my way as best I could towards the nearest point where nursing and doctoring could be had. It was one evening, in a lonely rest-hut on the edge of a huge forest, as I was waiting for my boy to bring the meal for which I was feverishly impatient, and which I knew I should loathe as soon as it was brought, that the explanation of the word 'Metskie' flashed on me. I had thought of it as referring to some Oriental potentate, some rebellious rajah perhaps, who was giving trouble, and whose followers had possibly discomfited an isolated British force in some out-of-the-way corner of our Empire. And all of a sudden I knew that 'Nemetskie Tsar,' German Emperor, had been the name that the man had been trying to convey to me. I shouted for the tracker, and put him through a breathless cross-examination; he confirmed what my fears had told me. The 'Metskie Tsar' was a big European ruler, he had been in conflict with the 'Angliskie Tsar,' and the latter had been defeated, swept away; the man spoke the word that he used for ships, and made energetic pantomime to express the sinking of a fleet. Holham, there was nothing for it but to hope that this was a false, groundless rumour, that had somehow crept to the confines of civilisation. In my saner balanced moments it was possible to disbelieve it, but if you have ever suffered from delirium you will know what raging torments of agony I went through in the nights, how my brain fought and refought that rumoured disaster."

The doctor gave a murmur of sympathetic understanding.

"Then," continued Yeovil, "I reached the small Siberian town towards which I had been struggling. There was a little colony of Russians there, traders, officials, a doctor or two, and some army officers. I put up at the primitive hotel-restaurant, which was the general gathering-place of the community. I knew quickly that the news was true. Russians are the most tactful of any European race that I have ever met; they did not stare with insolent or pitying curiosity, but there was something changed in their attitude which told me that the travelling Briton was no longer in their eyes the interesting respect-commanding personality that he had been in past days. I went to my own room, where the samovar was bubbling its familiar tune and a smiling red-shirted Russian boy was helping my Buriat servant to unpack my wardrobe, and I asked for any back numbers of newspapers that could be supplied at a moment's notice. I was given a bundle of well-thumbed sheets, odd pieces of the Novoe Vremya, the Moskovskie Viedomosti, one or two complete numbers of local papers published at Perm and Tobolsk. I do not read Russian well, though I speak it fairly readily, but from the fragments of disconnected telegrams that I pieced together I gathered enough information to acquaint me with the extent of the tragedy that had been worked out in a few crowded hours in a corner of North-Western Europe. I searched frantically for telegrams of later dates that would put a better complexion on the matter, that would retrieve something from the ruin; presently I came across a page of the illustrated supplement that the Novoe Vremya publishes once a week. There was a photograph of a long-fronted building with a flag flying over it, labelled 'The new standard floating over Buckingham Palace.' The picture was not much more than a smudge, but the flag, possibly touched up, was unmistakable. It was the eagle of the Nemetskie Tsar. I have a vivid recollection of that plainly-furnished little room, with the inevitable gilt ikon in one corner, and the samovar hissing and gurgling on the table, and the thrumming music of a balalaika orchestra coming up from the restaurant below; the next coherent thing I can remember was weeks and weeks later, discussing in an impersonal detached manner whether I was strong enough to stand the fatigue of the long railway journey to Finland.

"Since then, Holham, I have been encouraged to keep my mind as much off the war and public affairs as possible, and I have been glad to do so. I knew the worst and there was no particular use in deepening my despondency by dragging out the details. But now I am more or less a live man again, and I want to fill in the gaps in my knowledge of what happened. You know how much I know, and how little; those fragments of Russian newspapers were about all the information that I had. I don't even know clearly how the whole thing started."

Yeovil settled himself back in his chair with the air of a man who has done some necessary talking, and now assumes the role of listener.

"It started," said the doctor, "with a wholly unimportant disagreement about some frontier business in East Africa; there was a slight attack of nerves in the stock markets, and then the whole thing seemed in a fair way towards being settled. Then the negotiations over the affair began to drag unduly, and there was a further flutter of nervousness in the money world. And then one morning the papers reported a highly menacing speech by one of the German Ministers, and the situation began to look black indeed. 'He will be disavowed,' every one said over here, but in less than twenty-four hours those who knew anything knew that the crisis was on us—only their knowledge came too late. 'War between two such civilised and enlightened nations is an impossibility,' one of our leaders of public opinion had declared on the Saturday; by the following Friday the war had indeed become an impossibility, because we could no longer carry it on. It burst on us with calculated suddenness, and we were just not enough, everywhere where the pressure came. Our ships were good against their ships, our seamen were better than their seamen, but our ships were not able to cope with their ships plus their superiority in aircraft. Our trained men were good against their trained men, but they could not be in several places at once, and the enemy could. Our half-trained men and our untrained men could not master the science of war at a moment's notice, and a moment's notice was all they got. The enemy were a nation apprenticed in arms, we were not even the idle apprentice: we had not deemed apprenticeship worth our while. There was courage enough running loose in the land, but it was like unharnessed electricity, it controlled no forces, it struck no blows.

There was no time for the heroism and the devotion which a drawn-out struggle, however hopeless, can produce; the war was over almost as soon as it had begun. After the reverses which happened with lightning rapidity in the first three days of warfare, the newspapers made no effort to pretend that the situation could be retrieved; editors and public alike recognised that these were blows over the heart, and that it was a matter of moments before we were counted out. One might liken the whole affair to a snap checkmate early in a game of chess; one side had thought out the moves, and brought the requisite pieces into play, the other side was hampered and helpless, with its resources unavailable, its strategy discounted in advance. That, in a nutshell, is the history of the war."

Yeovil was silent for a moment or two, then he asked:

"And the sequel, the peace?"

"The collapse was so complete that I fancy even the enemy were hardly prepared for the consequences of their victory. No one had quite realised what one disastrous campaign would mean for an island nation with a closely packed population. The conquerors were in a position to dictate what terms they pleased, and it was not wonderful that their ideas of aggrandisement expanded in the hour of intoxication. There was no European combination ready to say them nay, and certainly no one Power was going to be rash enough to step in to contest the terms of the treaty that they imposed on the conquered. Annexation had probably never been a dream before the war; after the war it suddenly became temptingly practical. Warum nicht? became the theme of leader-writers in the German press; they pointed out that Britain, defeated and humiliated, but with enormous powers of recuperation, would be a dangerous and inevitable enemy for the Germany of tomorrow, while Britain incorporated within the Hohenzollern Empire would merely be a disaffected province, without a navy to make its disaffection a serious menace, and with great tax-paying capabilities, which would be available for relieving the burdens of the other Imperial States. Wherefore, why not annex? The warum nicht? party prevailed. Our King, as you know, retired with his Court to Delhi, as Emperor in the East, with most of his overseas dominions still subject to his sway. The British Isles came under the German Crown as a Reichsland, a sort of Alsace-Lorraine washed by the North Sea instead of the Rhine. We still retain our Parliament, but it is a clipped and pruned-down shadow of its former self, with most of its functions in abeyance; when the elections were held it was difficult to get decent candidates to come forward or to get people to vote. It makes one smile bitterly to think that a year or two ago we were seriously squabbling as to who should have votes. And, of course, the old party divisions have more or less crumbled away. The Liberals naturally are under the blackest of clouds, for having steered the country to disaster, though to do them justice it was no more their fault than the fault of any other party. In a democracy such as ours was the Government of the day must more or less reflect the ideas and temperament of the nation in all vital matters, and the British nation in those days could not have been persuaded of the urgent need for military apprenticeship or of the deadly nature of its danger. It was willing now and then to be half-frightened and to have half-measures, or, one might better say, quarter-measures taken to reassure it, and the governments of the day were willing to take them, but any political party or group of statesmen that had said 'the danger is enormous and immediate, the sacrifices and burdens must be enormous and immediate,' would have met with certain defeat at the polls. Still, of course, the Liberals, as the party that had held office for nearly a decade, incurred the odium of a people maddened by defeat and humiliation; one Minister, who had had less responsibility for military organisation than perhaps any of them, was attacked and nearly killed at Newcastle, another was hiding for three days on Exmoor, and escaped in disguise."

"And the Conservatives?"

"They are also under eclipse, but it is more or less voluntary in their case. For generations they had taken their stand as supporters of Throne and Constitution, and when they suddenly found the Constitution gone and the Throne filled by an alien dynasty, their political orientation had vanished. They are in much the same position as the Jacobites occupied after the Hanoverian accession. Many of the leading Tory families have emigrated to the British lands beyond the seas, others are shut up in their country houses, retrenching their expenses, selling their acres, and investing their money abroad. The Labour faction, again, are almost in as bad odour as the Liberals, because of having hob-nobbed too effusively and ostentatiously with the German democratic parties on the eve of the war, exploiting an evangel of universal brotherhood which did not blunt a single Teuton bayonet when the hour came. I suppose in time party divisions will reassert themselves in some form or other; there will be a Socialist Party, and the mercantile and manufacturing interests will evolve a sort of bourgeoise party, and the different religious bodies will try to get themselves represented—"

Yeovil made a movement of impatience.

"All these things that you forecast," he said, "must take time, considerable time; is this nightmare, then, to go on for ever?"

"It is not a nightmare, unfortunately," said the doctor, "it is a reality."

"But, surely—a nation such as ours, a virile, highly-civilised nation with an age-long tradition of mastery behind it, cannot be held under for ever by a few thousand bayonets and machine guns. We must surely rise up one day and drive them out."

"Dear man," said the doctor, "we might, of course, at some given moment overpower the garrison that is maintained here, and seize the forts, and perhaps we might be able to mine the harbours; what then? In a fortnight or so we could be starved into unconditional submission. Remember, all the advantages of isolated position that told in our favour while we had the sea dominion, tell against us now that the sea dominion is in other hands. The enemy would not need to mobilise a single army corps or to bring a single battleship into action; a fleet of nimble cruisers and destroyers circling round our coasts would be sufficient to shut out our food supplies."

"Are you trying to tell me that this is a final overthrow?" said Yeovil in a shaking voice; "are we to remain a subject race like the Poles?"

"Let us hope for a better fate," said the doctor. "Our opportunity may come if the Master Power is ever involved in an unsuccessful naval war with some other nation, or perhaps in some time of European crisis, when everything hung in the balance, our latent hostility might have to be squared by a concession of independence. That is what we have to hope for and watch for. On the other hand, the conquerors have to count on time and tact to weaken and finally obliterate the old feelings of nationality; the middle-aged of today will grow old and acquiescent in the changed state of things; the young generations will grow up never having known anything different. It's a far cry to Delhi, as the old Indian proverb says, and the strange half-European, half-Asiatic Court out there will seem more and more a thing exotic and unreal. 'The King across the water' was a rallying-cry once upon a time in our history, but a king on the further side of the Indian Ocean is a shadowy competitor for one who alternates between Potsdam and Windsor."

"I want you to tell me everything," said Yeovil, after another pause; "tell me, Holham, how far has this obliterating process of 'time and tact' gone? It seems to be pretty fairly started already. I bought a newspaper as soon as I landed, and I read it in the train coming up. I read things that puzzled and disgusted me. There were announcements of concerts and plays and first-nights and private views; there were even small dances. There were advertisements of house-boats and week-end cottages and string bands for garden parties. It struck me that it was rather like merrymaking with a dead body lying in the house."

"Yeovil," said the doctor, "you must bear in mind two things. First, the necessity for the life of the country going on as if nothing had happened. It is true that many thousands of our working men and women have emigrated and thousands of our upper and middle class too; they were the people who were not tied down by business, or who could afford to cut those ties. But those represent comparatively a few out of the many. The great businesses and the small businesses must go on, people must be fed and clothed and housed and medically treated, and their thousand-and-one wants and necessities supplied. Look at me, for instance; however much I loathe coming under a foreign domination and paying taxes to an alien government, I can't abandon my practice and my patients, and set up anew in Toronto or Allahabad, and if I could, some other doctor would have to take my place here. I or that other doctor must have our servants and motors and food and furniture and newspapers, even our sport. The golf links and the hunting field have been well-nigh deserted since the war, but they are beginning to get back their votaries because out-door sport has become a necessity, and a very rational necessity, with numbers of men who have to work otherwise under unnatural and exacting conditions. That is one factor of the situation. The other affects London more especially, but through London it influences the rest of the country to a certain extent. You will see around you here much that will strike you as indications of heartless indifference to the calamity that has befallen our nation. Well, you must remember that many things in modern life, especially in the big cities, are not national but international. In the world of music and art and the drama, for instance, the foreign names are legion, they confront you at every turn, and some of our British devotees of such arts are more acclimatised to the ways of Munich or Moscow than they are familiar with the life, say, of Stirling or York. For years they have lived and thought and spoken in an atmosphere and jargon of denationalised culture—even those of them who have never left our shores. They would take pains to be intimately familiar with the domestic affairs and views of life of some Galician gipsy dramatist, and gravely quote and discuss his opinions on debts and mistresses and cookery, while they would shudder at 'D'ye ken John Peel?' as a piece of uncouth barbarity. You cannot expect a world of that sort to be permanently concerned or downcast because the Crown of Charlemagne takes its place now on the top of the Royal box in the theatres, or at the head of programmes at State concerts. And then there are the Jews."

"There are many in the land, or at least in London," said Yeovil.

"There are even more of them now than there used to be," said Holham. "I am to a great extent a disliker of Jews myself, but I will be fair to them, and admit that those of them who were in any genuine sense British have remained British and have stuck by us loyally in our misfortune; all honour to them. But of the others, the men who by temperament and everything else were far more Teuton or Polish or Latin than they were British, it was not to be expected that they would be heartbroken because London had suddenly lost its place among the political capitals of the world, and became a cosmopolitan city. They had appreciated the free and easy liberty of the old days, under British rule, but there was a stiff insularity in the ruling race that they chafed against. Now, putting aside some petty Government restrictions that Teutonic bureaucracy has brought in, there is really, in their eyes, more licence and social adaptability in London than before. It has taken on some of the aspects of a No-Man's-Land, and the Jew, if he likes, may almost consider himself as of the dominant race; at any rate he is ubiquitous. Pleasure, of the cafe and cabaret and boulevard kind, the sort of thing that gave Berlin the aspect of the gayest capital in Europe within the last decade, that is the insidious leaven that will help to denationalise London. Berlin will probably climb back to some of its old austerity and simplicity, a world-ruling city with a great sense of its position and its responsibilities, while London will become more and more the centre of what these people understand by life."

Yeovil made a movement of impatience and disgust.

"I know, I know," said the doctor, sympathetically; "life and enjoyment mean to you the howl of a wolf in a forest, the call of a wild swan on the frozen tundras, the smell of a wood fire in some little inn among the mountains. There is more music to you in the quick thud, thud of hoofs on desert mud as a free-stepping horse is led up to your tent door than in all the dronings and flourishes that a highly-paid orchestra can reel out to an expensively fed audience. But the tastes of modern London, as we see them crystallised around us, lie in a very different direction. People of the world that I am speaking of, our dominant world at the present moment, herd together as closely packed to the square yard as possible, doing nothing worth doing, and saying nothing worth saying, but doing it and saying it over and over again, listening to the same melodies, watching the same artistes, echoing the same catchwords, ordering the same dishes in the same restaurants, suffering each other's cigarette smoke and perfumes and conversation, feverishly, anxiously making arrangements to meet each other again tomorrow, next week, and the week after next, and repeat the same gregarious experience. If they were not herded together in a corner of western London, watching each other with restless intelligent eyes, they would be herded together at Brighton or Dieppe, doing the same thing. Well, you will find that life of that sort goes forward just as usual, only it is even more prominent and noticeable now because there is less public life of other kinds."

Yeovil said something which was possibly the Buriat word for the nether world. Outside in the neighbouring square a band had been playing at intervals during the evening. Now it struck up an air that Yeovil had already heard whistled several times since his landing, an air with a captivating suggestion of slyness and furtive joyousness running through it.

He rose and walked across to the window, opening it a little wider. He listened till the last notes had died away.

"What is that tune they have just played?" he asked.

"You'll hear it often enough," said the doctor. "A Frenchman writing in the Matin the other day called it the 'National Anthem of the fait accompli.'"

IV

"Es Ist Verboten"

Yeovil wakened next morning to the pleasant sensation of being in a household where elaborate machinery for the smooth achievement of one's daily life was noiselessly and unceasingly at work. Fever and the long weariness of convalescence in indifferently comfortable surroundings had given luxury a new value in his eyes. Money had not always been plentiful with him in his younger days; in his twenty-eighth year he had inherited a fairly substantial fortune, and he had married a wealthy woman a few months later. It was characteristic of the man and his breed that the chief use to which he had put his newly-acquired wealth had been in seizing the opportunity which it gave him for indulging in unlimited travel in wild, out-of-the-way regions, where the comforts of life were meagrely represented. Cicely occasionally accompanied him to the threshold of his expeditions, such as Cairo or St. Petersburg or Constantinople, but her own tastes in the matter of roving were more or less condensed within an area that comprised Cannes, Homburg, the Scottish Highlands, and the Norwegian Fiords. Things outlandish and barbaric appealed to her chiefly when presented under artistic but highly civilised stage management on the boards of Covent Garden, and if she wanted to look at wolves or sand grouse, she preferred doing so in the company of an intelligent Fellow of the Zoological Society on some fine Sunday afternoon in Regent's Park. It was one of the bonds of union and good-fellowship between her husband and herself that each understood and sympathised with the other's tastes without in the least wanting to share them; they went their own ways and were pleased and comrade-like when the ways happened to run together for a span, without self-reproach or heart-searching when the ways diverged. Moreover, they had separate and adequate banking accounts, which constitute, if not the keys of the matrimonial Heaven, at least the oil that lubricates them.

Yeovil found Cicely and breakfast waiting for him in the cool breakfast-room, and enjoyed, with the appreciation of a recent invalid, the comfort and resources of a meal that had not to be ordered or thought about in advance, but seemed as though it were there, fore-ordained from the beginning of time in its smallest detail. Each desire of the breakfasting mind seemed to have its realisation in some dish, lurking unobtrusively in hidden corners until asked for. Did one want grilled mushrooms, English fashion, they were there, black and moist and sizzling, and extremely edible; did one desire mushrooms a la Russe, they appeared, blanched and cool and toothsome under their white blanketing of sauce. At one's bidding was a service of coffee, prepared with rather more forethought and circumspection than would go to the preparation of a revolution in a South American Republic.

The exotic blooms that reigned in profusion over the other parts of the house were scrupulously banished from the breakfast-room; bowls of wild thyme and other flowering weeds of the meadow and hedgerow gave it an atmosphere of country freshness that was in keeping with the morning meal.

"You look dreadfully tired still," said Cicely critically, "otherwise I would recommend a ride in the Park, before it gets too hot. There is a new cob in the stable that you will just love, but he is rather lively, and you had better content yourself for the present with some more sedate exercise than he is likely to give you. He is apt to try and jump out of his skin when the flies tease him. The Park is rather jolly for a walk just now."

"I think that will be about my form after my long journey," said Yeovil, "an hour's stroll before lunch under the trees. That ought not to fatigue me unduly. In the afternoon I'll look up one or two people."

"Don't count on finding too many of your old set," said Cicely rather hurriedly. "I dare say some of them will find their way back some time, but at present there's been rather an exodus."

"The Bredes," said Yeovil, "are they here?"

"No, the Bredes are in Scotland, at their place in Sutherlandshire; they don't come south now, and the Ricardes are farming somewhere in East Africa, the whole lot of them. Valham has got an appointment of some sort in the Straits Settlement, and has taken his family with him. The Collards are down at their mother's place in Norfolk; a German banker has bought their house in Manchester Square."

"And the Hebways?" asked Yeovil.

"Dick Hebway is in India," said Cicely, "but his mother lives in Paris; poor Hugo, you know, was killed in the war. My friends the Allinsons are in Paris too. It's rather a clearance, isn't it? However, there are some left, and I expect others will come back in time. Pitherby is here; he's one of those who are trying to make the best of things under the new regime."

"He would be," said Yeovil, shortly.

"It's a difficult question," said Cicely, "whether one should stay at home and face the music or go away and live a transplanted life under the British flag. Either attitude might be dictated by patriotism."

"It is one thing to face the music, it is another thing to dance to it," said Yeovil.

Cicely poured out some more coffee for herself and changed the conversation.

"You'll be in to lunch, I suppose? The Clubs are not very attractive just now, I believe, and the restaurants are mostly hot in the middle of the day. Ronnie Storre is coming in; he's here pretty often these days. A rather good-looking young animal with something mid-way between talent and genius in the piano-playing line."

"Not long-haired and Semetic or Tcheque or anything of that sort, I suppose?" asked Yeovil.

Cicely laughed at the vision of Ronnie conjured up by her husband's words.

"No, beautifully groomed and clipped and Anglo-Saxon. I expect you'll like him. He plays bridge almost as well as he plays the piano. I suppose you wonder at any one who can play bridge well wanting to play the piano."

"I'm not quite so intolerant as all that," said Yeovil; "anyhow I promise to like Ronnie. Is any one else coming to lunch?"

"Joan Mardle will probably drop in, in fact I'm afraid she's a certainty. She invited herself in that way of hers that brooks of no refusal. On the other hand, as a mitigating circumstance, there will be a point d'asperge omelette such as few kitchens could turn out, so don't be late."

Yeovil set out for his morning walk with the curious sensation of one who starts on a voyage of discovery in a land that is well known to him. He turned into the Park at Hyde Park corner and made his way along the familiar paths and alleys that bordered the Row. The familiarity vanished when he left the region of fenced-in lawns and rhododendron bushes and came to the open space that stretched away beyond the bandstand. The bandstand was still there, and a military band, in sky-blue Saxon uniform, was executing the first item in the forenoon programme of music. Around it, instead of the serried rows of green chairs that Yeovil remembered, was spread out an acre or so of small round tables, most of which had their quota of customers, engaged in a steady consumption of lager beer, coffee, lemonade and syrups. Further in the background, but well within earshot of the band, a gaily painted pagoda-restaurant sheltered a number of more commodious tables under its awnings, and gave a hint of convenient indoor accommodation for wet or windy weather. Movable screens of trellis-trained foliage and climbing roses formed little hedges by means of which any particular table could be shut off from its neighbours if semi-privacy were desired. One or two decorative advertisements of popularised brands of champagne and Rhine wines adorned the outside walls of the building, and under the central gable of its upper story was a flamboyant portrait of a stern-faced man, whose image and superscription might also be found on the newer coinage of the land. A mass of bunting hung in folds round the flag-pole on the gable, and blew out now and then on a favouring breeze, a long three-coloured strip, black, white, and scarlet, and over the whole scene the elm trees towered with an absurd sardonic air of nothing having changed around their roots.

Yeovil stood for a minute or two, taking in every detail of the unfamiliar spectacle.

"They have certainly accomplished something that we never attempted," he muttered to himself. Then he turned on his heel and made his way back to the shady walk that ran alongside the Row. At first sight little was changed in the aspect of the well-known exercising ground. One or two riding masters cantered up and down as of yore, with their attendant broods of anxious-faced young girls and awkwardly bumping women pupils, while horsey-looking men put marketable animals through their paces or drew up to the rails for long conversations with horsey-looking friends on foot. Sportingly attired young women, sitting astride of their horses, careered by at intervals as though an extremely game fox were leading hounds a merry chase a short way ahead of them; it all seemed much as usual.

Presently, from the middle distance a bright patch of colour set in a whirl of dust drew rapidly nearer and resolved itself into a group of cavalry officers extending their chargers in a smart gallop. They were well mounted and sat their horses to perfection, and they made a brave show as they raced past Yeovil with a clink and clatter and rhythmic thud, thud, of hoofs, and became once more a patch of colour in a whirl of dust. An answering glow of colour seemed to have burned itself into the grey face of the young man, who had seen them pass without appearing to look at them, a stinging rush of blood, accompanied by a choking catch in the throat and a hot white blindness across the eyes. The weakness of fever broke down at times the rampart of outward indifference that a man of Yeovil's temperament builds coldly round his heartstrings.

The Row and its riders had become suddenly detestable to the wanderer; he would not run the risk of seeing that insolently joyous cavalcade come galloping past again. Beyond a narrow stretch of tree-shaded grass lay the placid sunlit water of the Serpentine, and Yeovil made a short cut across the turf to reach its gravelled bank.

"Can't you read either English or German?" asked a policeman who confronted him as he stepped off the turf.

Yeovil stared at the man and then turned to look at the small neatly-printed notice to which the official was imperiously pointing; in two languages it was made known that it was forbidden and verboten, punishable and straffbar, to walk on the grass.

"Three shilling fine," said the policeman, extending his hand for the money.

"Do I pay you?" asked Yeovil, feeling almost inclined to laugh; "I'm rather a stranger to the new order of things."

"You pay me," said the policeman, "and you receive a quittance for the sum paid," and he proceeded to tear a counterfoil receipt for a three shilling fine from a small pocket book.

"May I ask," said Yeovil, as he handed over the sum demanded and received his quittance, "what the red and white band on your sleeve stands for?"

"Bi-lingual," said the constable, with an air of importance. "Preference is given to members of the Force who qualify in both languages. Nearly all the police engaged on Park duty are bi-lingual. About as many foreigners as English use the parks nowadays; in fact, on a fine Sunday afternoon, you'll find three foreigners to every two English. The park habit is more Continental than British, I take it."

"And are there many Germans in the police Force?" asked Yeovil.

"Well, yes, a good few; there had to be," said the constable; "there were such a lot of resignations when the change came, and they had to be filled up somehow. Lots of men what used to be in the Force emigrated or found work of some other kind, but everybody couldn't take that line; wives and children had to be thought of. 'Tisn't every head of a family that can chuck up a job on the chance of finding another. Starvation's been the lot of a good many what went out. Those of us that stayed on got better pay than we did before, but then of course the duties are much more multitudinous."

"They must be," said Yeovil, fingering his three shilling State document; "by the way," he asked, "are all the grass plots in the Park out of bounds for human feet?"

"Everywhere where you see the notices," said the policeman, "and that's about three-fourths of the whole grass space; there's been a lot of new gravel walks opened up in all directions. People don't want to walk on the grass when they've got clean paths to walk on."

And with this parting reproof the bi-lingual constable strode heavily away, his loss of consideration and self-esteem as a unit of a sometime ruling race evidently compensated for to some extent by his enhanced importance as an official.

"The women and children," thought Yeovil, as he looked after the retreating figure; "yes, that is one side of the problem. The children that have to be fed and schooled, the women folk that have to be cared for, an old mother, perhaps, in the home that cannot be broken up. The old case of giving hostages."

He followed the path alongside the Serpentine, passing under the archway of the bridge and continuing his walk into Kensington Gardens. In another moment he was within view of the Peter Pan statue and at once observed that it had companions. On one side was a group representing a scene from one of the Grimm fairy stories, on the other was Alice in conversation with Gryphon and Mockturtle, the episode looking distressingly stiff and meaningless in its sculptured form. Two other spaces had been cleared in the neighbouring turf, evidently for the reception of further statue groups, which Yeovil mentally assigned to Struwelpeter and Little Lord Fauntleroy.

"German middle-class taste," he commented, "but in this matter we certainly gave them a lead. I suppose the idea is that childish fancy is dead and that it is only decent to erect some sort of memorial to it."

The day was growing hotter, and the Park had ceased to seem a desirable place to loiter in. Yeovil turned his steps homeward, passing on his way the bandstand with its surrounding acreage of tables. It was now nearly one o'clock, and luncheon parties were beginning to assemble under the awnings of the restaurant. Lighter refreshments, in the shape of sausages and potato salads, were being carried out by scurrying waiters to the drinkers of lager beer at the small tables. A park orchestra, in brilliant trappings, had taken the place of the military band. As Yeovil passed the musicians launched out into the tune which the doctor had truly predicted he would hear to repletion before he had been many days in London; the "National Anthem of the fait accompli."

V

L'Art D'Etre Cousine

Joan Mardle had reached forty in the leisurely untroubled fashion of a woman who intends to be comely and attractive at fifty. She cultivated a jovial, almost joyous manner, with a top-dressing of hearty good will and good nature which disarmed strangers and recent acquaintances; on getting to know her better they hastily re-armed themselves. Some one had once aptly described her as a hedgehog with the protective mimicry of a puffball. If there was an awkward remark to be made at an inconvenient moment before undesired listeners, Joan invariably made it, and when the occasion did not present itself she was usually capable of creating it. She was not without a certain popularity, the sort of popularity that a dashing highwayman sometimes achieved among those who were not in the habit of travelling on his particular highway. A great-aunt on her mother's side of the family had married so often that Joan imagined herself justified in claiming cousin-ship with a large circle of disconnected houses, and treating them all on a relationship footing, which theoretical kinship enabled her to exact luncheons and other accommodations under the plea of keeping the lamp of family life aglow.

"I felt I simply had to come today," she chuckled at Yeovil; "I was just dying to see the returned traveller. Of course, I know perfectly well that neither of you want me, when you haven't seen each other for so long and must have heaps and heaps to say to one another, but I thought I would risk the odium of being the third person on an occasion when two are company and three are a nuisance. Wasn't it brave of me?"

She spoke in full knowledge of the fact that the luncheon party would not in any case have been restricted to Yeovil and his wife, having seen Ronnie arrive in the hall as she was being shown upstairs.

"Ronnie Storre is coming, I believe," said Cicely, "so you're not breaking into a tete-a-tete."

"Ronnie, oh I don't count him," said Joan gaily; "he's just a boy who looks nice and eats asparagus. I hear he's getting to play the piano really well. Such a pity. He will grow fat; musicians always do, and it will ruin him. I speak feelingly because I'm gravitating towards plumpness myself. The Divine Architect turns us out fearfully and wonderfully built, and the result is charming to the eye, and then He adds another chin and two or three extra inches round the waist, and the effect is ruined. Fortunately you can always find another Ronnie when this one grows fat and uninteresting; the supply of boys who look nice and eat asparagus is unlimited. Hullo, Mr. Storre, we were all talking about you."

"Nothing very damaging, I hope?" said Ronnie, who had just entered the room.

"No, we were merely deciding that, whatever you may do with your life, your chin must remain single. When one's chin begins to lead a double life one's own opportunities for depravity are insensibly narrowed. You needn't tell me that you haven't any hankerings after depravity; people with your coloured eyes and hair are always depraved."

"Let me introduce you to my husband, Ronnie," said Cicely, "and then let's go and begin lunch."

"You two must almost feel as if you were honeymooning again," said Joan as they sat down; "you must have quite forgotten each other's tastes and peculiarities since you last met. Old Emily Fronding was talking about you yesterday, when I mentioned that Murrey was expected home; 'curious sort of marriage tie,' she said, in that stupid staring way of hers, 'when husband and wife spend most of their time in different continents. I don't call it marriage at all.' 'Nonsense,' I said, 'it's the best way of doing things. The Yeovils will be a united and devoted couple long after heaps of their married contemporaries have trundled through the Divorce Court.' I forgot at the moment that her youngest girl had divorced her husband last year, and that her second girl is rumoured to be contemplating a similar step. One can't remember everything."

Joan Mardle was remarkable for being able to remember the smallest details in the family lives of two or three hundred acquaintances.

From personal matters she went with a bound to the political small talk of the moment.

"The Official Declaration as to the House of Lords is out at last," she said; "I bought a paper just before coming here, but I left it in the Tube. All existing titles are to lapse if three successive holders, including the present ones, fail to take the oath of allegiance."

"Have any taken it up to the present?" asked Yeovil.

"Only about nineteen, so far, and none of them representing very leading families; of course others will come in gradually, as the change of Dynasty becomes more and more an accepted fact, and of course there will be lots of new creations to fill up the gaps. I hear for certain that Pitherby is to get a title of some sort, in recognition of his literary labours. He has written a short history of the House of Hohenzollern, for use in schools you know, and he's bringing out a popular Life of Frederick the Great—at least he hopes it will be popular."

"I didn't know that writing was much in his line," said Yeovil, "beyond the occasional editing of a company prospectus."

"I understand his historical researches have given every satisfaction in exalted quarters," said Joan; "something may be lacking in the style, perhaps, but the august approval can make good that defect with the style of Baron. Pitherby has such a kind heart; 'kind hearts are more than coronets,' we all know, but the two go quite well together. And the dear man is not content with his services to literature, he's blossoming forth as a liberal patron of the arts. He's taken quite a lot of tickets for dear Gorla's debut; half the second row of the dress-circle."

"Do you mean Gorla Mustelford?" asked Yeovil, catching at the name; "what on earth is she having a debut about?"

"What?" cried Joan, in loud-voiced amazement; "haven't you heard? Hasn't Cicely told you? How funny that you shouldn't have heard. Why, it's going to be one of the events of the season. Everybody's talking about it. She's going to do suggestion dancing at the Caravansery Theatre."

"Good Heavens, what is suggestion dancing?" asked Yeovil.

"Oh, something quite new," explained Joan; "at any rate the name is quite new and Gorla is new as far as the public are concerned, and that is enough to establish the novelty of the thing. Among other things she does a dance suggesting the life of a fern; I saw one of the rehearsals, and to me it would have equally well suggested the life of John Wesley. However, that is probably the fault of my imagination—I've either got too much or too little. Anyhow it is an understood thing that she is to take London by storm."

"When I last saw Gorla Mustelford," observed Yeovil, "she was a rather serious flapper who thought the world was in urgent need of regeneration and was not certain whether she would regenerate it or take up miniature painting. I forget which she attempted ultimately."

"She is quite serious about her art," put in Cicely; "she's studied a good deal abroad and worked hard at mastering the technique of her profession. She's not a mere amateur with a hankering after the footlights. I fancy she will do well."

"But what do her people say about it?" asked Yeovil.

"Oh, they're simply furious about it," answered Joan; "the idea of a daughter of the house of Mustelford prancing and twisting about the stage for Prussian officers and Hamburg Jews to gaze at is a dreadful cup of humiliation for them. It's unfortunate, of course, that they should feel so acutely about it, but still one can understand their point of view."

"I don't see what other point of view they could possibly take," said Yeovil sharply; "if Gorla thinks that the necessities of art, or her own inclinations, demand that she should dance in public, why can't she do it in Paris or even Vienna? Anywhere would be better, one would think, than in London under present conditions."

He had given Joan the indication that she was looking for as to his attitude towards the fait accompli. Without asking a question she had discovered that husband and wife were divided on the fundamental issue that underlay all others at the present moment. Cicely was weaving social schemes for the future, Yeovil had come home in a frame of mind that threatened the destruction of those schemes, or at any rate a serious hindrance to their execution. The situation presented itself to Joan's mind with an alluring piquancy.

"You are giving a grand supper-party for Gorla on the night of her debut, aren't you?" she asked Cicely; "several people spoke to me about it, so I suppose it must be true."

Tony Luton and young Storre had taken care to spread the news of the projected supper function, in order to ensure against a change of plans on Cicely's part.

"Gorla is a great friend of mine," said Cicely, trying to talk as if the conversation had taken a perfectly indifferent turn; "also I think she deserves a little encouragement after the hard work she has been through. I thought it would be doing her a kindness to arrange a supper party for her on her first night."

There was a moment's silence. Yeovil said nothing, and Joan understood the value of being occasionally tongue-tied.

"The whole question is," continued Cicely, as the silence became oppressive, "whether one is to mope and hold aloof from the national life, or take our share in it; the life has got to go on whether we participate in it or not. It seems to me to be more patriotic to come down into the dust of the marketplace than to withdraw oneself behind walls or beyond the seas."

"Of course the industrial life of the country has to go on," said Yeovil; "no one could criticise Gorla if she interested herself in organising cottage industries or anything of that sort, in which she would be helping her own people. That one could understand, but I don't think a cosmopolitan concern like the music-hall business calls for personal sacrifices from young women of good family at a moment like the present."

"It is just at a moment like the present that the people want something to interest them and take them out of themselves," said Cicely argumentatively; "what has happened, has happened, and we can't undo it or escape the consequences. What we can do, or attempt to do, is to make things less dreary, and make people less unhappy."

"In a word, more contented," said Yeovil; "if I were a German statesman, that is the end I would labour for and encourage others to labour for, to make the people forget that they were discontented. All this work of regalvanising the social side of London life may be summed up in the phrase 'travailler pour le roi de Prusse.'"

"I don't think there is any use in discussing the matter further," said Cicely.

"I can see that grand supper-party not coming off," said Joan provocatively.

Ronnie looked anxiously at Cicely.

"You can see it coming on, if you're gifted with prophetic vision of a reliable kind," said Cicely; "of course as Murrey doesn't take kindly to the idea of Gorla's enterprise I won't have the party here. I'll give it at a restaurant, that's all. I can see Murrey's point of view, and sympathise with it, but I'm not going to throw Gorla over."

There was another pause of uncomfortably protracted duration.

"I say, this is a top-hole omelette," said Ronnie.

It was his only contribution to the conversation, but it was a valuable one.

VI

Herr von Kwarl

Herr von Kwarl sat at his favourite table in the Brandenburg Cafe, the new building that made such an imposing show (and did such thriving business) at the lower end of what most of its patrons called the Regentstrasse. Though the establishment was new it had already achieved its unwritten code of customs, and the sanctity of Herr von Kwarl's specially reserved table had acquired the authority of a tradition. A set of chessmen, a copy of the Kreuz Zeitung and the Times, and a slim-necked bottle of Rhenish wine, ice-cool from the cellar, were always to be found there early in the forenoon, and the honoured guest for whom these preparations were made usually arrived on the scene shortly after eleven o'clock. For an hour or so he would read and silently digest the contents of his two newspapers, and then at the first sign of flagging interest on his part, another of the cafe's regular customers would march across the floor, exchange a word or two on the affairs of the day, and be bidden with a wave of the hand into the opposite seat. A waiter would instantly place the chessboard with its marshalled ranks of combatants in the required position, and the contest would begin.

Herr von Kwarl was a heavily built man of mature middle-age, of the blond North-German type, with a facial aspect that suggested stupidity and brutality. The stupidity of his mien masked an ability and shrewdness that was distinctly above the average, and the suggestion of brutality was belied by the fact that von Kwarl was as kind-hearted a man as one could meet with in a day's journey. Early in life, almost before he was in his teens, Fritz von Kwarl had made up his mind to accept the world as it was, and to that philosophical resolution, steadfastly adhered to, he attributed his excellent digestion and his unruffled happiness. Perhaps he confused cause and effect; the excellent digestion may have been responsible for at least some of the philosophical serenity.

He was a bachelor of the type that is called confirmed, and which might better be labelled consecrated; from his early youth onward to his present age he had never had the faintest flickering intention of marriage. Children and animals he adored, women and plants he accounted somewhat of a nuisance. A world without women and roses and asparagus would, he admitted, be robbed of much of its charm, but with all their charm these things were tiresome and thorny and capricious, always wanting to climb or creep in places where they were not wanted, and resolutely drooping and fading away when they were desired to flourish. Animals, on the other hand, accepted the world as it was and made the best of it, and children, at least nice children, uncontaminated by grown-up influences, lived in worlds of their own making.

Von Kwarl held no acknowledged official position in the country of his residence, but it was an open secret that those responsible for the real direction of affairs sought his counsel on nearly every step that they meditated, and that his counsel was very rarely disregarded. Some of the shrewdest and most successful enactments of the ruling power were believed to have originated in the brain-cells of the bovine-fronted Stammgast of the Brandenburg Cafe.

Around the wood-panelled walls of the Cafe were set at intervals well-mounted heads of boar, elk, stag, roe-buck, and other game-beasts of a northern forest, while in between were carved armorial escutcheons of the principal cities of the lately expanded realm, Magdeburg, Manchester, Hamburg, Bremen, Bristol, and so forth. Below these came shelves on which stood a wonderful array of stone beer-mugs, each decorated with some fantastic device or motto, and most of them pertaining individually and sacredly to some regular and unfailing customer. In one particular corner of the highest shelf, greatly at his ease and in nowise to be disturbed, slept Wotan, the huge grey house-cat, dreaming doubtless of certain nimble and audacious mice down in the cellar three floors below, whose nimbleness and audacity were as precious to him as the forwardness of the birds is to a skilled gun on a grouse moor. Once every day Wotan came marching in stately fashion across the polished floor, halted mid-way to resume an unfinished toilet operation, and then proceeded to pay his leisurely respects to his friend von Kwarl. The latter was said to be prouder of this daily demonstration of esteem than of his many coveted orders of merit. Several of his friends and acquaintances shared with him the distinction of having achieved the Black Eagle, but not one of them had ever succeeded in obtaining the slightest recognition of their existence from Wotan.

The daily greeting had been exchanged and the proud grey beast had marched away to the music of a slumberous purr. The Kreuz Zeitung and the Times underwent a final scrutiny and were pushed aside, and von Kwarl glanced aimlessly out at the July sunshine bathing the walls and windows of the Piccadilly Hotel. Herr Rebinok, the plump little Pomeranian banker, stepped across the floor, almost as noiselessly as Wotan had done, though with considerably less grace, and some half-minute later was engaged in sliding pawns and knights and bishops to and fro on the chess-board in a series of lightning moves bewildering to look on. Neither he nor his opponent played with the skill that they severally brought to bear on banking and statecraft, nor did they conduct their game with the politeness that they punctiliously observed in other affairs of life. A running fire of contemptuous remarks and aggressive satire accompanied each move, and the mere record of the conversation would have given an uninitiated onlooker the puzzling impression that an easy and crushing victory was assured to both the players.

"Aha, he is puzzled. Poor man, he doesn't know what to do. . . Oho, he thinks he will move there, does he? Much good that will do him. . . Never have I seen such a mess as he is in. . . he cannot do anything, he is absolutely helpless, helpless."

"Ah, you take my bishop, do you? Much I care for that. Nothing. See, I give you check. Ah, now he is in a fright! He doesn't know where to go. What a mess he is in. . ."

So the game proceeded, with a brisk exchange of pieces and incivilities and a fluctuation of fortunes, till the little banker lost his queen as the result of an incautious move, and, after several woebegone contortions of his shoulders and hands, declined further contest. A sleek-headed piccolo rushed forward to remove the board, and the erstwhile combatants resumed the courteous dignity that they discarded in their chess-playing moments.

"Have you seen the Germania today?" asked Herr Rebinok, as soon as the boy had receded to a respectful distance.

"No," said von Kwarl, "I never see the Germania. I count on you to tell me if there is anything noteworthy in it."

"It has an article today headed, 'Occupation or Assimilation,'" said the banker. "It is of some importance, and well written. It is very pessimistic."

"Catholic papers are always pessimistic about the things of this world," said von Kwarl, "just as they are unduly optimistic about the things of the next world. What line does it take?"

"It says that our conquest of Britain can only result in a temporary occupation, with a 'notice to quit' always hanging over our heads; that we can never hope to assimilate the people of these islands in our Empire as a sort of maritime Saxony or Bavaria, all the teaching of history is against it; Saxony and Bavaria are part of the Empire because of their past history. England is being bound into the Empire in spite of her past history; and so forth."

"The writer of the article has not studied history very deeply," said von Kwarl. "The impossible thing that he speaks of has been done before, and done in these very islands, too. The Norman Conquest became an assimilation in comparatively few generations."

"Ah, in those days, yes," said the banker, "but the conditions were altogether different. There was not the rapid transmission of news and the means of keeping the public mind instructed in what was happening; in fact, one can scarcely say that the public mind was there to instruct. There was not the same strong bond of brotherhood between men of the same nation that exists now. Northumberland was almost as foreign to Devon or Kent as Normandy was. And the Church in those days was a great international factor, and the Crusades bound men together fighting under one leader for a common cause. Also there was not a great national past to be forgotten as there is in this case."

"There are many factors, certainly, that are against us," conceded the statesman, "but you must also take into account those that will help us. In most cases in recent history where the conquered have stood out against all attempts at assimilation, there has been a religious difference to add to the racial one—take Poland, for instance, and the Catholic parts of Ireland. If the Bretons ever seriously begin to assert their nationality as against the French, it will be because they have remained more Catholic in practice and sentiment than their neighbours. Here there is no such complication; we are in the bulk a Protestant nation with a Catholic minority, and the same may be said of the British. Then in modern days there is the alchemy of Sport and the Drama to bring men of different races amicably together. One or two sportsmanlike Germans in a London football team will do more to break down racial antagonism than anything that Governments or Councils can effect. As for the Stage, it has long been international in its tendencies. You can see that every day."

The banker nodded his head.

"London is not our greatest difficulty," continued von Kwarl. "You must remember the steady influx of Germans since the war; whole districts are changing the complexion of their inhabitants, and in some streets you might almost fancy yourself in a German town. We can scarcely hope to make much impression on the country districts and the provincial towns at present, but you must remember that thousands and thousands of the more virile and restless-souled men have emigrated, and thousands more will follow their example. We shall fill up their places with our own surplus population, as the Teuton races colonised England in the old pre-Christian days. That is better, is it not, to people the fat meadows of the Thames valley and the healthy downs and uplands of Sussex and Berkshire than to go hunting for elbow-room among the flies and fevers of the tropics? We have somewhere to go to, now, better than the scrub and the veldt and the thorn-jungles."

"Of course, of course," assented Herr Rebinok, "but while this desirable process of infiltration and assimilation goes on, how are you going to provide against the hostility of the conquered nation? A people with a great tradition behind them and the ruling instinct strongly developed, won't sit with their eyes closed and their hands folded while you carry on the process of Germanisation. What will keep them quiet?"

"The hopelessness of the situation. For centuries Britain has ruled the seas, and been able to dictate to half the world in consequence; then she let slip the mastery of the seas, as something too costly and onerous to keep up, something which aroused too much jealousy and uneasiness in others, and now the seas rule her. Every wave that breaks on her shore rattles the keys of her prison. I am no fire-eater, Herr Rebinok, but I confess that when I am at Dover, say, or Southampton, and see those dark blots on the sea and those grey specks in the sky, our battleships and cruisers and aircraft, and realise what they mean to us my heart beats just a little quicker. If every German was flung out of England tomorrow, in three weeks' time we should be coming in again on our own terms. With our sea scouts and air scouts spread in organised network around, not a shipload of foodstuff could reach the country. They know that; they can calculate how many days of independence and starvation they could endure, and they will make no attempt to bring about such a certain fiasco. Brave men fight for a forlorn hope, but the bravest do not fight for an issue they know to be hopeless."

"That is so," said Herr Rebinok, "as things are at present they can do nothing from within, absolutely nothing. We have weighed all that beforehand. But, as the Germania points out, there is another Britain beyond the seas. Supposing the Court at Delhi were to engineer a league—"

"A league? A league with whom?" interrupted the statesman. "Russia we can watch and hold. We are rather nearer to its western frontier than Delhi is, and we could throttle its Baltic trade at five hours' notice. France and Holland are not inclined to provoke our hostility; they would have everything to lose by such a course."

"There are other forces in the world that might be arrayed against us," argued the banker; "the United States, Japan, Italy, they all have navies."

"Does the teaching of history show you that it is the strong Power, armed and ready, that has to suffer from the hostility of the world?" asked von Kwarl. "As far as sentiment goes, perhaps, but not in practice. The danger has always been for the weak, dismembered nation. Think you a moment, has the enfeebled scattered British Empire overseas no undefended territories that are a temptation to her neighbours? Has Japan nothing to glean where we have harvested? Are there no North American possessions which might slip into other keeping? Has Russia herself no traditional temptations beyond the Oxus? Mind you, we are not making the mistake Napoleon made, when he forced all Europe to be for him or against him. We threaten no world aggressions, we are satiated where he was insatiable. We have cast down one overshadowing Power from the face of the world, because it stood in our way, but we have made no attempt to spread our branches over all the space that it covered. We have not tried to set up a tributary Canadian republic or to partition South Africa; we have dreamed no dream of making ourselves Lords of Hindostan. On the contrary, we have given proof of our friendly intentions towards our neighbours. We backed France up the other day in her squabble with Spain over the Moroccan boundaries, and proclaimed our opinion that the Republic had as indisputable a mission on the North Africa coast as we have in the North Sea. That is not the action or the language of aggression. No," continued von Kwarl, after a moment's silence, "the world may fear us and dislike us, but, for the present at any rate, there will be no leagues against us. No, there is one rock on which our attempt at assimilation will founder or find firm anchorage."

"And that is—?"

"The youth of the country, the generation that is at the threshold now. It is them that we must capture. We must teach them to learn, and coax them to forget. In course of time Anglo-Saxon may blend with German, as the Elbe Saxons and the Bavarians and Swabians have blended with the Prussians into a loyal united people under the sceptre of the

Hohenzollerns. Then we should be doubly strong, Rome and Carthage rolled into one, an Empire of the West greater than Charlemagne ever knew. Then we could look Slav and Latin and Asiatic in the face and keep our place as the central dominant force of the civilised world."

The speaker paused for a moment and drank a deep draught of wine, as though he were invoking the prosperity of that future world-power. Then he resumed in a more level tone:

"On the other hand, the younger generation of Britons may grow up in hereditary hatred, repulsing all our overtures, forgetting nothing and forgiving nothing, waiting and watching for the time when some weakness assails us, when some crisis entangles us, when we cannot be everywhere at once. Then our work will be imperilled, perhaps undone. There lies the danger, there lies the hope, the younger generation."

"There is another danger," said the banker, after he had pondered over von Kwarl's remarks for a moment or two amid the incense-clouds of a fat cigar; "a danger that I foresee in the immediate future; perhaps not so much a danger as an element of exasperation which may ultimately defeat your plans. The law as to military service will have to be promulgated shortly, and that cannot fail to be bitterly unpopular. The people of these islands will have to be brought into line with the rest of the Empire in the matter of military training and military service, and how will they like that? Will not the enforcing of such a measure enfuriate them against us? Remember, they have made great sacrifices to avoid the burden of military service."

"Dear God," exclaimed Herr von Kwarl, "as you say, they have made sacrifices on that altar!"

VII

The Lure

Cicely had successfully insisted on having her own way concerning the projected supper-party; Yeovil had said nothing further in opposition to it, whatever his feelings on the subject might be. Having gained her point, however, she was anxious to give her husband the impression of having been consulted, and to put her victory as far as possible on the footing of a compromise. It was also rather a relief to be able to discuss the matter out of range of Joan's disconcerting tongue and observant eyes.

"I hope you are not really annoyed about this silly supper-party," she said on the morning before the much-talked-of first night. "I had pledged myself to give it, so I couldn't back out without seeming mean to Gorla, and in any case it would have been impolitic to cry off."

"Why impolitic?" asked Yeovil coldly.

"It would give offence in quarters where I don't want to give offence," said Cicely.

"In quarters where the fait accompli is an object of solicitude," said Yeovil.

"Look here," said Cicely in her most disarming manner, "it's just as well to be perfectly frank about the whole matter. If one wants to live in the London of the present day one must make up one's mind to accept the fait accompli with as good a grace as possible. I do want to live in London, and I don't want to change my way of living and start under different conditions in some other place. I can't face the prospect of tearing up my life by the roots; I feel certain that I shouldn't bear transplanting. I can't imagine myself recreating my circle of interests in some foreign town or colonial centre or even in a country town in England. India I couldn't stand. London is not merely a home to me, it is a world, and it happens to be just the world that suits me and that I am suited to. The German occupation, or whatever one likes to call it, is a calamity, but it's not like a molten deluge from Vesuvius that need send us all scuttling away from another Pompeii. Of course," she added, "there are things that jar horribly on one, even when one has got more or less accustomed to them, but one must just learn to be philosophical and bear them."

"Supposing they are not bearable?" said Yeovil; "during the few days that I've been in the land I've seen things that I cannot imagine will ever be bearable."

"That is because they're new to you," said Cicely.

"I don't wish that they should ever come to seem bearable," retorted Yeovil. "I've been bred and reared as a unit of a ruling race; I don't want to find myself settling down resignedly as a member of an enslaved one."

"There's no need to make things out worse than they are," protested Cicely. "We've had a military disaster on a big scale, and there's been a great political dislocation in consequence. But there's no reason why everything shouldn't right itself in time, as it has done after other similar disasters in the history of nations. We are not scattered to the winds or wiped off the face of the earth, we are still an important racial unit."

"A racial unit in a foreign Empire," commented Yeovil.

"We may arrive at the position of being the dominant factor in that Empire," said Cicely, "impressing our national characteristics on it, and perhaps dictating its dynastic future and the whole trend of its policy. Such things have happened in history. Or we may become strong enough to throw off the foreign connection at a moment when it can be done effectually and advantageously. But meanwhile it is necessary to preserve our industrial life and our social life, and for that reason we must accommodate ourselves to present circumstances, however distasteful they may be. Emigration to some colonial wilderness, or holding ourselves rigidly aloof from the life of the capital, won't help matters. Really, Murrey, if you will think things over a bit, you will see that the course I am following is the one dictated by sane patriotism."

"Whom the gods wish to render harmless they first afflict with sanity," said Yeovil bitterly. "You may be content to wait for a hundred years or so, for this national revival to creep and crawl us back into a semblance of independence and world-importance. I'm afraid I haven't the patience or the philosophy to sit down comfortably and wait for a change of fortune that won't come in my time—if it comes at all."

Cicely changed the drift of the conversation; she had only introduced the argument for the purpose of defining her point of view and accustoming Yeovil to it, as one leads a nervous horse up to an unfamiliar barrier that he is required eventually to jump.

"In any case," she said, "from the immediately practical standpoint England is the best place for you till you have shaken off all traces of that fever. Pass the time away somehow till the hunting begins, and then go down to the East Wessex country; they are looking out for a new master after this season, and if you were strong enough you might take it on for a while. You could go to Norway for fishing in the summer and hunt the East Wessex in the winter. I'll come down and do a bit of hunting too, and we'll have house-parties, and get a little golf in between whiles. It will be like old times."

Yeovil looked at his wife and laughed.

"Who was that old fellow who used to hunt his hounds regularly through the fiercest times of the great Civil War? There is a picture of him, by Caton Woodville, I think, leading his pack between King Charles's army and the Parliament forces just as some battle was going to begin. I have often thought that the King must have disliked him rather more than he disliked the men who were in arms against him; they at least cared, one way or the other. I fancy that old chap would have a great many imitators nowadays, though, when it came to be a question of sport against soldiering. I don't know whether anyone has said it, but one might almost assert that the German victory was won on the golf-links of Britain."

"I don't see why you should saddle one particular form of sport with a special responsibility," protested Cicely.

"Of course not," said Yeovil, "except that it absorbed perhaps more of the energy and attention of the leisured class than other sports did, and in this country the leisured class was the only bulwark we had against official indifference. The working classes had a big share of the apathy, and, indirectly, a greater share of the responsibility, because the voting power was in their hands. They had not the leisure, however, to sit down and think clearly what the danger was; their own industrial warfare was more real to them than anything that was threatening from the nation that they only knew from samples of German clerks and German waiters."

"In any case," said Cicely, "as regards the hunting, there is no Civil War or national war raging just now, and there is no immediate likelihood of one. A good many hunting seasons will have to come and go before we can think of a war of independence as even a distant possibility, and in the meantime hunting and horse-breeding and country sports generally are the things most likely to keep Englishmen together on the land. That is why so many men who hate the German occupation are trying to keep field sports alive, and in the right hands. However, I won't go on arguing. You and I always think things out for ourselves and decide for ourselves, which is much the best way in the long run."

Cicely slipped away to her writing-room to make final arrangements over the telephone for the all-important supper-party, leaving Yeovil to turn over in his mind the suggestion that she had thrown out. It was an obvious lure, a lure to draw him away from the fret and fury that possessed him so inconveniently, but its obvious nature did not detract from its effectiveness. Yeovil had pleasant recollections of the East Wessex, a cheery little hunt that afforded good sport in an unpretentious manner, a joyous thread of life running through a rather sleepy countryside, like a merry brook careering through a placid valley. For a man coming slowly and yet eagerly back to the activities of life from the weariness of a long fever, the prospect of a leisurely season with the East Wessex was singularly attractive, and side by side with its attractiveness there was a tempting argument in favour of yielding to its attractions. Among the small squires and yeoman farmers, doctors, country tradesmen, auctioneers and so forth who would gather at the covert-side and at the hunt breakfasts, there might be a local nucleus of revolt against the enslavement of the land, a discouraged and leaderless band waiting for some one to mould their resistance into effective shape and keep their loyalty to the old dynasty and the old national cause steadily burning. Yeovil could see himself taking up that position, stimulating the spirit of hostility to the fait accompli, organising stubborn opposition to every Germanising influence that was brought into play, schooling the youth of the countryside to look steadily Delhiward. That was the bait that Yeovil threw out to his conscience, while slowly considering the other bait that was appealing so strongly to his senses. The dry warm scent of the stable, the nip of the morning air, the pleasant squelch-squelch of the saddle leather, the moist earthy fragrance of the autumn woods and wet fallows, the cold white mists of winter days, the whimper of hounds and the hot restless pushing of the pack through ditch and hedgerow and undergrowth, the birds that flew up and clucked and chattered as you passed, the hearty greeting and pleasant gossip in farmhouse kitchens and market-day bar-parlours—all these remembered delights of the chase marshalled themselves in the brain, and made a cumulative appeal that came with special intensity to a man who was a little tired of his wanderings, more than a little drawn away from the jarring centres of life. The hot London sunshine baking the soot-grimed walls and the ugly incessant hoot and grunt of the motor traffic gave an added charm to the vision of hill and hollow and copse that flickered in Yeovil's mind. Slowly, with a sensuous lingering over detail, his imagination carried him down to a small, sleepy, yet withal pleasantly bustling market town, and placed him unerringly in a wide straw-littered yard, half-full of men and quarter-full of horses, with a bob-tailed sheep-dog or two trying not to get in everybody's way, but insisting on being in the thick of things. The horses gradually detached themselves from the crowd of unimportant men and came one by one into momentary prominence, to be discussed and appraised for their good points and bad points, and finally to be bid for. And always there was one horse that detached itself conspicuously from the rest, the ideal hunter, or at any rate, Yeovil's ideal of the ideal hunter. Mentally it was put through its paces before him, its pedigree and brief history recounted to him; mentally he saw a stable lad put it over a jump or two, with credit to all concerned, and inevitably he saw himself outbidding less discerning rivals and securing the desired piece of horseflesh, to be the chief glory and mainstay of his hunting stable, to carry him well and truly and cleverly through many a joyous long-to-be-remembered run. That scene had been one of the recurring half-waking dreams of his long days of weakness in the far-away Finnish nursing-home, a dream sometimes of tantalising mockery, sometimes of pleasure in the foretaste of a joy to come. And now it need scarcely be a dream any longer, he had only to go down at the right moment and take an actual part in his oft-rehearsed vision. Everything would be there, exactly as his imagination had placed it, even down to the bob-tailed sheep-dogs; the horse of his imagining would be there waiting for him, or if not absolutely the ideal animal, something very like it. He might even go beyond the limits of his dream and pick up a couple of desirable animals—there would probably be fewer purchasers for good class hunters in these days than of yore. And with the coming of this reflection his dream faded suddenly and his mind came back with a throb of pain to the things he had for the moment forgotten, the weary, hateful things that were symbolised for him by the standard that floated yellow and black over the frontage of Buckingham Palace.

Yeovil wandered down to his snuggery, a mood of listless dejection possessing him. He fidgetted aimlessly with one or two books and papers, filled a pipe, and half filled a waste-paper basket with torn circulars and accumulated writing-table litter. Then he lit the pipe and settled down in his most comfortable armchair with an old note-book in his hand. It was a sort of disjointed diary, running fitfully through the winter months of some past years, and recording noteworthy days with the East Wessex.

And over the telephone Cicely talked and arranged and consulted with men and women to whom the joys of a good gallop or the love of a stricken fatherland were as letters in an unknown alphabet.

VIII

The First-Night

Huge posters outside the Caravansery Theatre of Varieties announced the first performance of the uniquely interesting Suggestion Dances, interpreted by the Hon. Gorla Mustelford. An impressionist portrait of a rather severe-looking young woman gave the public some idea of what the danseuse might be like in appearance, and the further information was added that her performance was the greatest dramatic event of the season. Yet another piece of information was conveyed to the public a few minutes after the doors had opened, in the shape of large notices bearing the brief announcement, "house full." For the first-night function most of the seats had been reserved for specially-invited guests or else bespoken by those who considered it due to their own importance to be visible on such an occasion.

Even at the commencement of the ordinary programme of the evening (Gorla was not due to appear till late in the list) the theatre was crowded with a throng of chattering, expectant human beings; it seemed as though every one had come early to see every one else arrive. As a matter of fact it was the rumour-heralded arrival of one personage in particular that had drawn people early to their seats and given a double edge to the expectancy of the moment.

At first sight and first hearing the bulk of the audience seemed to comprise representatives of the chief European races in well-distributed proportions, but if one gave it closer consideration it could be seen that the distribution was geographically rather than ethnographically diversified. Men and women there were from Paris, Munich, Rome, Moscow and Vienna, from Sweden and Holland and divers other cities and countries, but in the majority of cases the Jordan Valley had supplied their forefathers with a common cradle-ground. The lack of a fire burning on a national altar seemed to have drawn them by universal impulse to the congenial flare of the footlights, whether as artists, producers, impresarios, critics, agents, go-betweens, or merely as highly intelligent and fearsomely well-informed spectators. They were prominent in the chief seats, they were represented, more sparsely but still in fair numbers, in the cheaper places, and everywhere they were voluble, emphatic, sanguine or sceptical, prodigal of word and gesture, with eyes that seemed to miss nothing and acknowledge nothing, and a general restless dread of not being seen and noticed. Of the theatre-going London public there was also a fair muster, more particularly centred in the less expensive parts of the house, while in boxes, stalls and circles a sprinkling of military uniforms gave an unfamiliar tone to the scene in the eyes of those who had not previously witnessed a first-night performance under the new conditions.

Yeovil, while standing aloof from his wife's participation in this social event, had made private arrangements for being a personal spectator of the scene; as one of the ticket-buying public he had secured a seat in the back row of a low-priced gallery, whence he might watch, observant and unobserved, the much talked-of debut of Gorla Mustelford, and the writing of a new chapter in the history of the fait accompli. Around him he noticed an incessant undercurrent of jangling laughter, an unending give-and-take of meaningless mirthless jest and catchword. He had noticed the same thing in streets and public places since his arrival in London, a noisy, empty interchange of chaff and laughter that he had been at a loss to account for. The Londoner is not well adapted for the irresponsible noisiness of jesting tongue that bubbles up naturally in a Southern race, and the effort to be volatile was the more noticeable because it so obviously was an effort. Turning over the pages of a book that told the story of Bulgarian social life in the days of Turkish rule, Yeovil had that morning come across a passage that seemed to throw some light on the thing that had puzzled him:

"Bondage has this one advantage: it makes a nation merry. Where far-reaching ambition has no scope for its development the community squanders its energy on the trivial and personal cares of its daily life, and seeks relief and recreation in simple and easily obtained material enjoyment." The writer was a man who had known bondage, so he spoke at any rate with authority. Of the London of the moment it could not, however, be said with any truth that it was merry, but merely that its inhabitants made desperate endeavour not to appear crushed under their catastrophe. Surrounded as he was now with a babble of tongues and shrill mechanical repartee, Yeovil's mind went back to the book and its account of a theatre audience in the Turkish days of Bulgaria, with its light and laughing crowd of critics and spectators. Bulgaria! The thought of that determined little nation came to him with a sharp sense of irony. There was a people who had not thought it beneath the dignity of their manhood to learn the trade and discipline of arms. They had their reward; torn and exhausted and debt-encumbered from their campaigns, they were masters in their own house, the Bulgarian flag flew over the Bulgarian mountains. And Yeovil stole a glance at the crown of Charlemagne set over the Royal box.

In a capacious box immediately opposite the one set aside for royalty the Lady Shalem sat in well-considered prominence, confident that every press critic and reporter would note her presence, and that one or two of them would describe, or misdescribe, her toilet. Already quite a considerable section of the audience knew her by name, and the frequency with which she graciously nodded towards various quarters of the house suggested the presence of a great many personal acquaintances. She had attained to that desirable feminine altitude of purse and position when people who go about everywhere know you well by sight and have never met your dress before.

Lady Shalem was a woman of commanding presence, of that type which suggests a consciousness that the command may not necessarily be obeyed; she had observant eyes and a well-managed voice. Her successes in life had been worked for, but they were also to some considerable extent the result of accident. Her public history went back to the time when, in the person of her husband, Mr. Conrad Dort, she had contested two hopeless and very expensive Parliamentary elections on behalf of her party; on each occasion the declaration of the poll had shown a heavy though reduced majority on the wrong side, but she might have perpetrated an apt misquotation of the French monarch's traditional message after the defeat of Pavia, and assured the world "all is lost save honours." The forthcoming Honours List had duly proclaimed the fact that Conrad Dort, Esquire, had entered Parliament by another door as Baron Shalem, of Wireskiln, in the county of Suffolk. Success had crowned the lady's efforts as far as the achievement of the title went, but her social ambitions seemed unlikely to make further headway. The new Baron and his wife, their title and money notwithstanding, did not "go down" in their particular segment of county society, and in London there were other titles and incomes to compete with. People were willing to worship the Golden Calf, but allowed themselves a choice of altars. No one could justly say that the Shalems were either oppressively vulgar or insufferably bumptious; probably the chief reason for their lack of popularity was their intense and obvious desire to be popular. They kept open house in such an insistently open manner that they created a social draught. The people who accepted their invitations for the second or third time were not the sort of people whose names gave importance to a dinner party or a house gathering. Failure, in a thinly-disguised form, attended the assiduous efforts of the Shalems to play a leading role in the world that they had climbed into. The Baron began to observe to his acquaintances that "gadding about" and entertaining on a big scale was not much in his line; a quiet after-dinner pipe and talk with some brother legislator was his ideal way of spending an evening.

Then came the great catastrophe, involving the old order of society in the national overthrow. Lady Shalem, after a decent interval of patriotic mourning, began to look around her and take stock of her chances and opportunities under the new regime. It was easier to achieve distinction as a titled oasis in the social desert that London had become than it had been to obtain recognition as a new growth in a rather overcrowded field. The observant eyes and agile brain quickly noted this circumstance, and her ladyship set to work to adapt herself to the altered conditions that governed her world. Lord Shalem was one of the few Peers who kissed the hand of the new Sovereign, his wife was one of the few hostesses who attempted to throw a semblance of gaiety and lavish elegance over the travesty of a London season following the year of disaster. The world of tradesmen and purveyors and caterers, and the thousands who were dependent on them for employment, privately blessed the example set by Shalem House, whatever their feelings might be towards the fait accompli, and the august newcomer who had added an old Saxon kingdom and some of its accretions to the Teutonic realm of Charlemagne was duly beholden to an acquired subject who was willing to forget the bitterness of defeat and to help others to forget it also. Among other acts of Imperial recognition an earldom was being held in readiness for the Baron who had known how to accept accomplished facts with a good grace. One of the wits of the Cockatrice Club had asserted that the new earl would take as supporters for his coat of arms a lion and a unicorn oublie.

In the box with Lady Shalem was the Grafin von Tolb, a well-dressed woman of some fifty-six years, comfortable and placid in appearance, yet alert withal, rather suggesting a thoroughly wide-awake dormouse. Rich, amiable and intelligent were the adjectives which would best have described her character and her life-story. In her own rather difficult social circle at Paderborn she had earned for herself the reputation of being one of the most tactful and discerning hostesses in Germany, and it was generally suspected that she had come over and taken up her residence in London in response to a wish expressed in high quarters; the lavish hospitality which she dispensed at her house in Berkeley Square was a considerable reinforcement to the stricken social life of the metropolis.

In a neighbouring box Cicely Yeovil presided over a large and lively party, which of course included Ronnie Storre, who was for once in a way in a chattering mood, and also included an American dowager, who had never been known to be in anything else. A tone of literary distinction was imparted to the group by the presence of Augusta Smith, better known under her pen-name of Rhapsodic Pantril, author of a play that had had a limited but well-advertised success in Sheffield and the United States of America, author also of a book of reminiscences, entitled "Things I Cannot Forget." She had beautiful eyes, a knowledge of how to dress, and a pleasant disposition, cankered just a little by a perpetual dread of the non-recognition of her genius. As the woman, Augusta Smith, she probably would have been unreservedly happy; as the super-woman, Rhapsodic Pantril, she lived within the border-line of discontent. Her most ordinary remarks were framed with the view of arresting attention; some one once said of her that she ordered a sack of potatoes with the air of one who is making enquiry for a love-philtre.

"Do you see what colour the curtain is?" she asked Cicely, throwing a note of intense meaning into her question.

Cicely turned quickly and looked at the drop-curtain.

"Rather a nice blue," she said.

"Alexandrine blue—my colour—the colour of hope," said Rhapsodie impressively.

"It goes well with the general colour-scheme," said Cicely, feeling that she was hardly rising to the occasion.

"Say, is it really true that His Majesty is coming?" asked the lively American dowager. "I've put on my nooest frock and my best diamonds on purpose, and I shall be mortified to death if he doesn't see them."

"There!" pouted Ronnie, "I felt certain you'd put them on for me."

"Why no, I should have put on rubies and orange opals for you. People with our colour of hair always like barbaric display—"

"They don't," said Ronnie, "they have chaste cold tastes. You are absolutely mistaken."

"Well, I think I ought to know!" protested the dowager; "I've lived longer in the world than you have, anyway."

"Yes," said Ronnie with devastating truthfulness, "but my hair has been this colour longer than yours has."

Peace was restored by the opportune arrival of a middle-aged man of blond North-German type, with an expression of brutality on his rather stupid face, who sat in the front of the box for a few minutes on a visit of ceremony to Cicely. His appearance caused a slight buzz of recognition among the audience, and if Yeovil had cared to make enquiry of his neighbours he might have learned that this decorated and obviously important personage was the redoubtable von Kwarl, artificer and shaper of much of the statecraft for which other men got the public credit.

The orchestra played a selection from the "Gondola Girl," which was the leading musical-comedy of the moment. Most of the audience, those in the more expensive seats at any rate, heard the same airs two or three times daily, at restaurant lunches, teas, dinners and suppers, and occasionally in the Park; they were justified therefore in treating the music as a background to slightly louder conversation than they had hitherto indulged in. The music came to an end, episode number two in the evening's entertainment was signalled, the curtain of Alexandrine blue rolled heavily upward, and a troupe of performing wolves was presented to the public. Yeovil had encountered wolves in North Africa deserts and in Siberian forest and wold, he had seen them at twilight stealing like dark shadows across the snow, and heard their long whimpering howl in the darkness amid the pines; he could well understand how a magic lore had grown up round them through the ages among the peoples of four continents, how their name had passed into a hundred strange sayings and inspired a hundred traditions. And now he saw them ride round the stage on tricycles, with grotesque ruffles round their necks and clown caps on their heads, their eyes blinking miserably in the blaze of the footlights. In response to the applause of the house a stout, atrociously smiling man in evening dress came forward and bowed; he had had nothing to do either with the capture or the training of the animals, having bought them ready for use from a continental emporium where wild beasts were prepared for the music-hall market, but he continued bowing and smiling till the curtain fell.

Two American musicians with comic tendencies (denoted by the elaborate rags and tatters of their costumes) succeeded the wolves. Their musical performance was not without merit, but their comic "business" seemed to have been invented long ago by some man who had patented a monopoly of all music-hall humour and forthwith retired from the trade. Some day, Yeovil reflected, the rights of the monopoly might expire and new "business" become available for the knockabout profession.

The audience brightened considerably when item number five of the programme was signalled. The orchestra struck up a rollicking measure and Tony Luton made his entrance amid a rousing storm of applause. He was dressed as an errand-boy of some West End shop, with a livery and box-tricycle, as spruce and decorative as the most ambitious errand-boy could see himself in his most ambitious dreams. His song was a lively and very audacious chronicle of life behind the scenes of a big retail establishment, and sparkled with allusions which might fitly have been described as suggestive—at any rate they appeared to suggest meanings to the audience quite as clearly as Gorla Mustelford's dances were likely to do, even with the aid, in her case, of long explanations on the programmes. When the final verse seemed about to reach an unpardonable climax a stage policeman opportunely appeared and moved the lively songster on for obstructing the imaginary traffic of an imaginary Bond Street. The house received the new number with genial enthusiasm, and mingled its applause with demands for an earlier favourite. The orchestra struck up the familiar air, and in a few moments the smart errand-boy, transformed now into a smart jockey, was singing "They quaff the gay bubbly in Eccleston Square" to an audience that hummed and nodded its unstinted approval.

The next number but one was the Gorla Mustelford debut, and the house settled itself down to yawn and fidget and chatter for ten or twelve minutes while a troupe of talented Japanese jugglers performed some artistic and quite uninteresting marvels with fans and butterflies and lacquer boxes. The interval of waiting was not destined, however, to be without its interest; in its way it provided the one really important and dramatic moment of the evening. One or two uniforms and evening toilettes had already made their appearance in the Imperial box; now there was observable in that quarter a slight commotion, an unobtrusive reshuffling and reseating, and then every eye in the suddenly quiet semi-darkened house focussed itself on one figure. There was no public demonstration from the newly-loyal, it had been particularly wished that there should be none, but a ripple of whisper went through the vast audience from end to end. Majesty had arrived. The Japanese marvel-workers went through their display with even less attention than before. Lady Shalem, sitting well in the front of her box, lowered her observant eyes to her programme and her massive bangles. The evidence of her triumph did not need staring at.

IX

An Evening "To Be Remembered"

To the uninitiated or unappreciative the dancing of Gorla Mustelford did not seem widely different from much that had been exhibited aforetime by exponents of the posturing school. She was not naturally graceful of movement, she had not undergone years of arduous tutelage, she had not the instinct for sheer joyous energy of action that is stored in some natures; out of these unpromising negative qualities she had produced a style of dancing that might best be labelled a conscientious departure from accepted methods. The highly imaginative titles that she had bestowed on her dances, the "Life of a fern," the "Soul-dream of a topaz," and so forth, at least gave her audience and her critics something to talk about. In themselves they meant absolutely nothing, but they induced discussion, and that to Gorla meant a great deal. It was a season of dearth and emptiness in the footlights and box-office world, and her performance received a welcome that would scarcely have befallen it in a more crowded and prosperous day. Her success, indeed, had been waiting for her, ready-made, as far as the managerial profession was concerned, and nothing had been left undone in the way of advertisement to secure for it the appearance, at any rate, of popular favour. And loud above the interested applause of those who had personal or business motives for acclaiming a success swelled the exaggerated enthusiasm of the fairly numerous art-satellites who are unstinted in their praise of anything that they are certain they cannot understand. Whatever might be the subsequent verdict of the theatre-filling public the majority of the favoured first-night audience was determined to set the seal of its approval on the suggestion dances, and a steady roll of applause greeted the conclusion of each item. The dancer gravely bowed her thanks; in marked contradistinction to the gentleman who had "presented" the performing wolves she did not permit herself the luxury of a smile.

"It teaches us a great deal," said Rhapsodic Pantril vaguely, but impressively, after the Fern dance had been given and applauded.

"At any rate we know now that a fern takes life very seriously," broke in Joan Mardle, who had somehow wriggled herself into Cicely's box.

As Yeovil, from the back of his gallery, watched Gorla running and ricochetting about the stage, looking rather like a wagtail in energetic pursuit of invisible gnats and midges, he wondered how many of the middle-aged women who were eagerly applauding her would have taken the least notice of similar gymnastics on the part of their offspring in nursery or garden, beyond perhaps asking them not to make so much noise. And a bitterer tinge came to his thoughts as he saw the bouquets being handed up, thoughts of the brave old dowager down at Torywood, the woman who had worked and wrought so hard and so unsparingly in her day for the well-being of the State—the State that had fallen helpless into alien hands before her tired eyes. Her eldest son lived invalid-wise in the South of France, her second son lay fathoms deep in the North Sea, with the hulk of a broken battleship for a burial-vault; and now the grand-daughter was standing here in the limelight, bowing her thanks for the patronage and favour meted out to her by this cosmopolitan company, with its lavish sprinkling of the uniforms of an alien army.

Prominent among the flowers at her feet was one large golden-petalled bouquet of gorgeous blooms, tied with a broad streamer of golden riband, the tribute rendered by Caesar to the things that were Caesar's. The new chapter of the fait accompli had been written that night and written well. The audience poured slowly out with the triumphant music of Jancovius's Kaiser Wilhelm march, played by the orchestra as a happy inspiration, pealing in its ears.

"It has been a great evening, a most successful evening," said Lady Shalem to Herr von Kwarl, whom she was conveying in her electric brougham to Cicely Yeovil's supper party; "an important evening," she added, choosing her adjectives with deliberation. "It should give pleasure in high quarters, should it not?"

And she turned her observant eyes on the impassive face of her companion.

"Gracious lady," he replied with deliberation and meaning, "it has given pleasure. It is an evening to be remembered."

The gracious lady suppressed a sigh of satisfaction. Memory in high places was a thing fruitful and precious beyond computation.

Cicely's party at the Porphyry Restaurant had grown to imposing dimensions. Every one whom she had asked had come, and so had Joan Mardle. Lady Shalem had suggested several names at the last moment, and there was quite a strong infusion of the Teutonic military and official world. It was just as well, Cicely reflected, that the supper was being given at a restaurant and not in Berkshire Street.

"Quite like ole times," purred the beaming proprietor in Cicely's ear, as the staircase and cloak-rooms filled up with a jostling, laughing throng.

The guests settled themselves at four tables, taking their places where chance or fancy led them, late comers having to fit in wherever they could find room. A babel of tongues in various languages reigned round the tables, amid which the rattle of knives and forks and plates and the popping of corks made a subdued hubbub. Gorla Mustelford, the motive for all this sound and movement, this chatter of guests and scurrying of waiters, sat motionless in the fatigued self-conscious silence of a great artist who has delivered a great message.

"Do sit at Lady Peach's table, like a dear boy," Cicely begged of Tony Luton, who had come in late; "she and Gerald Drowly have got together, in spite of all my efforts, and they are both so dull. Try and liven things up a bit."

A loud barking sound, as of fur-seals calling across Arctic ice, came from another table, where Mrs. Mentieth-Mendlesohnn (one of the Mendlesohnns of Invergordon, as she was wont to describe herself) was proclaiming the glories and subtleties of Gorla's achievement.

"It was a revelation," she shouted; "I sat there and saw a whole new scheme of thought unfold itself before my eyes. One could not define it, it was thought translated into action—the best art cannot be defined. One just sat there and knew that one was seeing something one had never seen before, and yet one felt that one had seen it, in one's brain, all one's life. That was what was so wonderful—yes, please," she broke off sharply as a fat quail in aspic was presented to her by a questioning waiter.

The voice of Mr. Mauleverer Morle came across the table, like another seal barking at a greater distance.

"Rostand," he observed with studied emphasis, "has been called le Prince de l'adjectif Inopine; Miss Mustelford deserves to be described as the Queen of Unexpected Movement."

"Oh, I say, do you hear that?" exclaimed Mrs. Mentieth-Mendlesohnn to as wide an audience as she could achieve; "Rostand has been called—tell them what you said, Mr. Morle," she broke off, suddenly mistrusting her ability to handle a French sentence at the top of her voice.

Mr. Morle repeated his remark.

"Pass it on to the next table," commanded Mrs. Mentieth-Mendlesohnn. "It's too good to be lost."

At the next table however, a grave impressive voice was dwelling at length on a topic remote from the event of the evening. Lady Peach considered that all social gatherings, of whatever nature, were intended for the recital of minor domestic tragedies. She lost no time in regaling the company around her with the detailed history of an interrupted week-end in a Norfolk cottage.

"The most charming and delightful old-world spot that you could imagine, clean and quite comfortable, just a nice distance from the sea and within an easy walk of the Broads. The very place for the children. We'd brought everything for a four days' stay and meant to have a really delightful time. And then on Sunday morning we found that some one had left the springhead, where our only supply of drinking water came from, uncovered, and a dead bird was floating in it; it had fallen in somehow and got drowned. Of course we couldn't use the water that a dead body had been floating in, and there was no other supply for miles round, so we had to come away then and there. Now what do you say to that?"

"'Ah, that a linnet should die in the Spring,'" quoted Tony Luton with intense feeling.

There was an immediate outburst of hilarity where Lady Peach had confidently looked for expressions of concern and sympathy.

"Isn't Tony just perfectly cute? Isn't he?" exclaimed a young American woman, with an enthusiasm to which Lady Peach entirely failed to respond. She had intended following up her story with the account of another tragedy of a similar nature that had befallen her three years ago in Argyllshire, and now the opportunity had gone. She turned morosely to the consolations of a tongue salad.

At the centre table the excellent von Tolb led a chorus of congratulation and compliment, to which Gorla listened with an air of polite detachment, much as the Sheikh Ul Islam might receive the homage of a Wesleyan Conference. To a close observer it would have seemed probable that her attitude of fatigued indifference to the flattering remarks that were showered on her had been as carefully studied and rehearsed as any of her postures on the stage.

"It is something that one will appreciate more and more fully every time one sees it. . . One cannot see it too often. . . I could have sat and watched it for hours. . . Do you know, I am just looking forward to tomorrow evening, when I can see it again. . . I knew it was going to be good, but I had no idea—" so chimed the chorus, between mouthfuls of quail and bites of asparagus.

"Weren't the performing wolves wonderful?" exclaimed Joan in her fresh joyous voice, that rang round the room like laughter of the woodpecker.

If there is one thing that disturbs the complacency of a great artist of the Halls it is the consciousness of sharing his or her triumphs with performing birds and animals, but of course Joan was not to be expected to know that. She pursued her subject with the assurance of one who has hit on a particularly acceptable topic.

"It must have taken them years of training and concentration to master those tricycles," she continued in high-pitched soliloquy. "The nice thing about them is that they don't realise a bit how clever and educational they are. It would be dreadful to have them putting on airs, wouldn't it? And yet I suppose the knowledge of being able to jump through a hoop better than any other wolf would justify a certain amount of 'side.'"

Fortunately at this moment a young Italian journalist at another table rose from his seat and delivered a two-minute oration in praise of the heroine of the evening. He spoke in rapid nervous French, with a North Italian accent, but much of what he said could be understood by the majority of those present, and the applause was unanimous. At any rate he had been brief and it was permissible to suppose that he had been witty.

It was the opening for which Mr. Gerald Drowly had been watching and waiting. The moment that the Italian enthusiast had dropped back into his seat amid a rattle of hand-clapping and rapping of forks and knives on the tables, Drowly sprang to his feet, pushed his chair well away, as for a long separation, and begged to endorse what had been so very aptly and gracefully, and, might he add, truly said by the previous speaker. This was only the prelude to the real burden of his message; with the dexterity that comes of practice he managed, in a couple of hurried sentences, to divert the course of his remarks to his own personality and career, and to inform his listeners that he was an actor of some note and experience, and had had the honour of acting under—and here followed a string of names of eminent actor managers of the day. He thought he might be pardoned for mentioning the fact that his performance of "Peterkin" in the "Broken Nutshell," had won the unstinted approval of the dramatic critics of the Provincial press. Towards the end of what was a long speech, and which seemed even longer to its hearers, he reverted to the subject of Gorla's dancing and bestowed on it such laudatory remarks as he had left over. Drawing his chair once again into his immediate neighbourhood he sat down, aglow with the satisfied consciousness of a good work worthily performed.

"I once acted a small part in some theatricals got up for a charity," announced Joan in a ringing, confidential voice; "the Clapham Courier said that all the minor parts were very creditably sustained. Those were its very words. I felt I must tell you that, and also say how much I enjoyed Miss Mustelford's dancing."

Tony Luton cheered wildly.

"That's the cleverest speech so far," he proclaimed. He had been asked to liven things up at his table and was doing his best to achieve that result, but Mr. Gerald Drowly joined Lady Peach in the unfavourable opinion she had formed of that irrepressible youth.

Ronnie, on whom Cicely kept a solicitous eye, showed no sign of any intention of falling in love with Gorla. He was more profitably engaged in paying court to the Grafin von Tolb, whose hospitable mansion in Belgrave Square invested her with a special interest in his eyes. As a professional Prince Charming he had every inducement to encourage the cult of Fairy Godmother.

"Yes, yes, agreed, I will come and hear you play, that is a promise," said the Grafin, "and you must come and dine with me one night and play to me afterwards, that is a promise, also, yes? That is very nice of you, to come and see a tiresome old woman. I am passionately fond of music; if I were honest I would tell you also that I am very fond of good-looking boys, but this is not the age of honesty, so I must leave you to guess that. Come on Thursday in next week, you can? That is nice. I have a reigning Prince dining with me that night. Poor man, he wants cheering up; the art of being a reigning Prince is not a very pleasing one nowadays. He has made it a boast all his life that he is Liberal and his subjects Conservative; now that is all changed—no, not all; he is still Liberal, but his subjects unfortunately are become Socialists. You must play your best for him."

"Are there many Socialists over there, in Germany I mean?" asked Ronnie, who was rather out of his depth where politics were concerned.

"Ueberall," said the Grafin with emphasis; "everywhere, I don't know what it comes from; better education and worse digestions I suppose. I am sure digestion has a good deal to do with it. In my husband's family for example, his generation had excellent digestions, and there wasn't a case of Socialism or suicide among them; the younger generation have no digestions worth speaking of, and there have been two suicides and three Socialists within the last six years. And now I must really be going. I am not a Berliner and late hours don't suit my way of life."

Ronnie bent low over the Grafin's hand and kissed it, partly because she was the kind of woman who naturally invoked such homage, but chiefly because he knew that the gesture showed off his smooth burnished head to advantage.

The observant eyes of Lady Shalem had noted the animated conversation between the Grafin and Ronnie, and she had overheard fragments of the invitation that had been accorded to the latter.

"Take us the little foxes, the little foxes that spoil the vines," she quoted to herself; "not that that music-boy would do much in the destructive line, but the principle is good."

X

Some Reflections and a "Te Deum"

Cicely awoke, on the morning after the "memorable evening," with the satisfactory feeling of victory achieved, tempered by a troubled sense of having achieved it in the face of a reasonably grounded opposition. She had burned her boats, and was glad of it, but the reek of their burning drifted rather unpleasantly across the jubilant incense-swinging of her Te Deum service.

Last night had marked an immense step forward in her social career; without running after the patronage of influential personages she had seen it quietly and tactfully put at her service. People such as the Grafin von Tolb were going to be a power in the London world for a very long time to come. Herr von Kwarl, with all his useful qualities of brain and temperament, might conceivably fall out of favour in some unexpected turn of the political wheel, and the Shalems would probably have their little day and then a long afternoon of diminishing social importance; the placid dormouse-like Grafin would outlast them all. She had the qualities which make either for contented mediocrity or else for very durable success, according as circumstances may dictate. She was one of those characters that can neither thrust themselves to the front, nor have any wish to do so, but being there, no ordinary power can thrust them away.

With the Grafin as her friend Cicely found herself in altogether a different position from that involved by the mere interested patronage of Lady Shalem. A vista of social success was opened up to her, and she did not mean it to be just the ordinary success of a popular and influential hostess moving in an important circle. That people with naturally bad manners should have to be polite and considerate in their dealings with her, that people who usually held themselves aloof should have to be gracious and amiable, that the self-assured should have to be just a little humble and anxious where she was concerned, these things of course she intended to happen; she was a woman. But, she told herself, she intended a great deal more than that when she traced the pattern for her scheme of social influence. In her heart she detested the German occupation as a hateful necessity, but while her heart registered the hatefulness the brain recognised the necessity. The great fighting-machines that the Germans had built up and maintained, on land, on sea, and in air, were three solid crushing facts that demonstrated the hopelessness of any immediate thought of revolt. Twenty years hence, when the present generation was older and greyer, the chances of armed revolt would probably be equally hopeless, equally remote-seeming. But in the meantime something could have been effected in another way. The conquerors might partially Germanise London, but, on the other hand, if the thing were skilfully managed, the British element within the Empire might impress the mark of its influence on everything German. The fighting men might remain Prussian or Bavarian, but the thinking men, and eventually the ruling men, could gradually come under British influence, or even be of British blood. An English Liberal-Conservative "Centre" might stand as a bulwark against the Junkerdom and Socialism of Continental Germany. So Cicely reasoned with herself, in a fashion induced perhaps by an earlier apprenticeship to the reading of Nineteenth Century articles, in which the possible political and racial developments of various countries were examined and discussed and put away in the pigeon-holes of probable happenings. She had sufficient knowledge of political history to know that such a development might possibly come to pass, she had not sufficient insight into actual conditions to know that the possibility was as remote as that of armed resistance. And the role which she saw herself playing was that of a deft and courtly political intriguer, rallying the British element and making herself agreeable to the German element, a political inspiration to the one and a social distraction to the other. At the back of her mind there lurked an honest confession that she was probably over-rating her powers of statecraft and personality, that she was more likely to be carried along by the current of events than to control or divert its direction; the political day-dream remained, however, as day-dreams will, in spite of the clear light of probability shining through them. At any rate she knew, as usual, what she wanted to do, and as usual she had taken steps to carry out her intentions. Last night remained in her mind a night of important victory. There also remained the anxious proceeding of finding out if the victory had entailed any serious losses.

Cicely was not one of those ill-regulated people who treat the first meal of the day as a convenient occasion for serving up any differences or contentions that have been left over from the day before or overlooked in the press of other matters. She enjoyed her breakfast and gave Yeovil unhindered opportunity for enjoying his; a discussion as to the right cooking of a dish that he had first tasted among the Orenburg Tartars was the prevailing topic on this particular morning, and blended well with trout and toast and coffee. In a cosy nook of the smoking-room, in participation of the after-breakfast cigarettes, Cicely made her dash into debatable ground.

"You haven't asked me how my supper-party went off," she said.

"There is a notice of it in two of the morning papers, with a list of those present," said Yeovil; "the conquering race seems to have been very well represented."

"Several races were represented," said Cicely; "a function of that sort, celebrating a dramatic first-night, was bound to be cosmopolitan. In fact, blending of races and nationalities is the tendency of the age we live in."

"The blending of races seems to have been consummated already in one of the individuals at your party," said Yeovil drily; "the name Mentieth-Mendlesohnn struck me as a particularly happy obliteration of racial landmarks."

Cicely laughed.

"A noisy and very wearisome sort of woman," she commented; "she reminds one of garlic that's been planted by mistake in a conservatory. Still, she's useful as an advertising agent to any one who rubs her the right way. She'll be invaluable in proclaiming the merits of Gorla's performance to all and sundry; that's why I invited her. She'll probably lunch today at the Hotel Cecil, and every one sitting within a hundred yards of her table will hear what an emotional education they can get by going to see Gorla dance at the Caravansery."

"She seems to be like the Salvation Army," said Yeovil; "her noise reaches a class of people who wouldn't trouble to read press notices."

"Exactly," said Cicely. "Gorla gets quite good notices on the whole, doesn't she?"

"The one that took my fancy most was the one in the Standard," said Yeovil, picking up that paper from a table by his side and searching its columns for the notice in question. "'The wolves which appeared earlier in the evening's entertainment are, the programme assures us, trained entirely by kindness. It would have been a further kindness, at any rate to the audience, if some of the training, which the wolves doubtless do not appreciate at its proper value, had been expended on Miss Mustelford's efforts at stage dancing. We are assured, again on the authority of the programme, that the much-talked-of Suggestion Dances are the last word in Posture dancing. The last word belongs by immemorial right to the sex which Miss Mustelford adorns, and it would be ungallant to seek to deprive her of her privilege. As far as the educational aspect of her performance is concerned we must admit that the life of the fern remains to us a private life still. Miss Mustelford has abandoned her own private life in an unavailing attempt to draw the fern into the gaze of publicity. And so it was with her other suggestions. They suggested many things, but nothing that was announced on the programme. Chiefly they suggested one outstanding reflection, that stage-dancing is not like those advertised breakfast foods that can be served up after three minutes' preparation. Half a life-time, or rather half a youth-time is a much more satisfactory allowance.'"

"The Standard is prejudiced," said Cicely; "some of the other papers are quite enthusiastic. The Dawn gives her a column and a quarter of notice, nearly all of it complimentary. It says the report of her fame as a dancer went before her, but that her performance last night caught it up and outstripped it."

"I should not like to suggest that the Dawn is prejudiced," said Yeovil, "but Shalem is a managing director on it, and one of its biggest shareholders. Gorla's dancing is an event of the social season, and Shalem is one of those most interested in keeping up the appearance, at any rate, of a London social season. Besides, her debut gave the opportunity for an Imperial visit to the theatre—the first appearance at a festive public function of the Conqueror among the conquered. Apparently the experiment passed off well; Shalem has every reason to feel pleased with himself and well-disposed towards Gorla. By the way," added Yeovil, "talking of Gorla, I'm going down to Torywood one day next week."

"To Torywood?" exclaimed Cicely. The tone of her exclamation gave the impression that the announcement was not very acceptable to her.

"I promised the old lady that I would go and have a talk with her when I came back from my Siberian trip; she travelled in eastern Russia, you know, long before the Trans-Siberian railway was built, and she's enormously interested in those parts. In any case I should like to see her again."

"She does not see many people nowadays," said Cicely; "I fancy she is breaking up rather. She was very fond of the son who went down, you know."

"She has seen a great many of the things she cared for go down," said Yeovil; "it is a sad old life that is left to her, when one thinks of all that the past has been to her, of the part she used to play in the world, the work she used to get through. It used to seem as though she could never grow old, as if she would die standing up, with some unfinished command on her lips. And now I suppose her tragedy is that she has grown old, bitterly old, and cannot die."

Cicely was silent for a moment, and seemed about to leave the room. Then she turned back and said:

"I don't think I would say anything about Gorla to her if I were you."

"It would not have occurred to me to drag her name into our conversation," said Yeovil coldly, "but in any case the accounts of her dancing performance will have reached Torywood through the newspapers—also the record of your racially-blended supper-party."

Cicely said nothing. She knew that by last night's affair she had definitely identified herself in public opinion with the Shalem clique, and that many of her old friends would look on her with distrust and suspicion on that account. It was unfortunate, but she reckoned it a lesser evil than tearing herself away from her London life, its successes and pleasures and possibilities. These social dislocations and severing of friendships were to be looked for after any great and violent change in State affairs. It was Yeovil's attitude that really troubled her; she would not give way to his prejudices and accept his point of view, but she knew that a victory that involved estrangement from him would only bring a mockery of happiness. She still hoped that he would come round to an acceptance of established facts and deaden his political malaise in the absorbing distraction of field sports. The visit to Torywood was a misfortune; it might just turn the balance in the undesired direction. Only a few weeks of late summer and early autumn remained before the hunting season, and its preparations would be at hand, and Yeovil might be caught in the meshes of an old enthusiasm; in those few weeks, however, he might be fired by another sort of enthusiasm, an enthusiasm which would sooner or later mean voluntary or enforced exile for his part, and the probable breaking up of her own social plans and ambitions.

But Cicely knew something of the futility of improvising objections where no real obstacle exists. The visit to Torywood was a graceful attention on Yeovil's part to an old friend; there was no decent ground on which it could be opposed. If the influence of that visit came athwart Yeovil's life and hers with disastrous effect, that was "Kismet."

And once again the reek from her burned and smouldering boats mingled threateningly with the incense fumes of her Te Deum for victory. She left the room, and Yeovil turned once more to an item of news in the morning's papers that had already arrested his attention. The Imperial Aufklarung on the subject of military service was to be made public in the course of the day.

XI

The Tea Shop

Yeovil wandered down Piccadilly that afternoon in a spirit of restlessness and expectancy. The long-awaited Aufklarung dealing with the new law of military service had not yet appeared; at any moment he might meet the hoarse-throated newsboys running along with their papers, announcing the special edition which would give the terms of the edict to the public. Every sound or movement that detached itself with isolated significance from the general whirr and scurry of the streets seemed to Yeovil to herald the oncoming clamour and rush that he was looking for. But the long endless succession of motors and 'buses and vans went by, hooting and grunting, and such newsboys as were to be seen hung about listlessly, bearing no more attractive bait on their posters than the announcement of an "earthquake shock in Hungary: feared loss of life."

The Green Park end of Piccadilly was a changed, and in some respects a livelier thoroughfare to that which Yeovil remembered with affectionate regret. A great political club had migrated from its palatial home to a shrunken habitation in a less prosperous quarter; its place was filled by the flamboyant frontage of the Hotel Konstantinopel. Gorgeous Turkey carpets were spread over the wide entrance steps, and boys in Circassian and Anatolian costumes hung around the doors, or dashed forth in un-Oriental haste to carry such messages as the telephone was unable to transmit. Picturesque sellers of Turkish delight, attar-of-roses, and brass-work coffee services, squatted under the portico, on terms of obvious good understanding with the hotel management. A few doors further down a service club that had long been a Piccadilly landmark was a landmark still, as the home of the Army Aeronaut Club, and there was a constant coming and going of gay-hued uniforms, Saxon, Prussian, Bavarian, Hessian, and so forth, through its portals. The mastering of the air and the creation of a scientific aerial war fleet, second to none in the world, was an achievement of which the conquering race was pardonably proud, and for which it had good reason to be duly thankful. Over the gateways was blazoned the badge of the club, an elephant, whale, and eagle, typifying the three armed forces of the State, by land and sea and air; the eagle bore in its beak a scroll with the proud legend: "The last am I, but not the least."

To the eastward of this gaily-humming hive the long shuttered front of a deserted ducal mansion struck a note of protest and mourning amid the noise and whirl and colour of a seemingly uncaring city. On the other side of the roadway, on the gravelled paths of the Green Park, small ragged children from the back streets of Westminster looked wistfully at the smooth trim stretches of grass on which it was now forbidden, in two languages, to set foot. Only the pigeons, disregarding the changes of political geography, walked about as usual, wondering perhaps, if they ever wondered at anything, at the sudden change in the distribution of park humans.

Yeovil turned his steps out of the hot sunlight into the shade of the Burlington Arcade, familiarly known to many of its newer frequenters as the Passage. Here the change that new conditions and requirements had wrought was more immediately noticeable than anywhere else in the West End. Most of the shops on the western side had been cleared away, and in their place had been installed an "open-air" cafe, converting the long alley into a sort of promenade tea-garden, flanked on one side by a line of haberdashers', perfumers', and jewellers' show windows. The patrons of the cafe could sit at the little round tables, drinking their coffee and syrups and aperitifs, and gazing, if they were so minded, at the pyjamas and cravats and Brazilian diamonds spread out for inspection before them. A string orchestra, hidden away somewhere in a gallery, was alternating grand opera with the Gondola Girl and the latest gems of Transatlantic melody. From around the tightly-packed tables arose a babble of tongues, made up chiefly of German, a South American rendering of Spanish, and a North American rendering of English, with here and there the sharp shaken-out staccato of Japanese. A sleepy-looking boy, in a nondescript uniform, was wandering to and fro among the customers, offering for sale the Matin, New York Herald, Berliner Tageblatt, and a host of crudely coloured illustrated papers, embodying the hard-worked wit of a world-legion of comic artists. Yeovil hurried through the Arcade; it was not here, in this atmosphere of staring alien eyes and jangling tongues, that he wanted to read the news of the Imperial Aufklarung.

By a succession of by-ways he reached Hanover Square, and thence made his way into Oxford Street. There was no commotion of activity to be noticed yet among the newsboys; the posters still concerned themselves with the earthquake in Hungary, varied with references to the health of the King of Roumania, and a motor accident in South London. Yeovil wandered aimlessly along the street for a few dozen yards, and then turned down into the smoking-room of a cheap tea-shop, where he judged that the flourishing foreign element would be less conspicuously represented. Quiet-voiced, smooth-headed youths, from neighbouring shops and wholesale houses, sat drinking tea and munching pastry, some of them reading, others making a fitful rattle with dominoes on the marble-topped tables. A clean, wholesome smell of tea and coffee made itself felt through the clouds of cigarette smoke; cleanliness and listlessness seemed to be the dominant notes of the place, a cleanliness that was commendable, and a listlessness that seemed unnatural and undesirable where so much youth was gathered together for refreshment and recreation. Yeovil seated himself at a table already occupied by a young clergyman who was smoking a cigarette over the remains of a plateful of buttered toast. He had a keen, clever, hard-lined face, the face of a man who, in an earlier stage of European history, might have been a warlike prior, awkward to tackle at the council-board, greatly to be avoided where blows were being exchanged. A pale, silent damsel drifted up to Yeovil and took his order with an air of being mentally some hundreds of miles away, and utterly indifferent to the requirements of those whom she served; if she had brought calf's-foot jelly instead of the pot of China tea he had asked for, Yeovil would hardly have been surprised. However, the tea duly arrived on the table, and the pale damsel scribbled a figure on a slip of paper, put it silently by the side of the teapot, and drifted silently away. Yeovil had seen the same sort of thing done on the musical-comedy stage, and done rather differently.

"Can you tell me, sir, is the Imperial announcement out yet?" asked the young clergyman, after a brief scrutiny of his neighbour.

"No, I have been waiting about for the last half-hour on the look-out for it," said Yeovil; "the special editions ought to be out by now." Then he added: "I have only just lately come from abroad. I know scarcely anything of London as it is now. You may imagine that a good deal of it is very strange to me. Your profession must take you a good deal among all classes of people. I have seen something of what one may call the upper, or, at any rate, the richer classes, since I came back; do tell me something about the poorer classes of the community. How do they take the new order of things?"

"Badly," said the young cleric, "badly, in more senses than one. They are helpless and they are bitter—bitter in the useless kind of way that produces no great resolutions. They look round for some one to blame for what has happened; they blame the politicians, they blame the leisured classes; in an indirect way I believe they blame the Church. Certainly, the national disaster has not drawn them towards religion in any form. One thing you may be sure of, they do not blame themselves. No true Londoner ever admits that fault lies at his door. 'No, I never!' is an exclamation that is on his lips from earliest childhood, whenever he is charged with anything blameworthy or punishable. That is why school discipline was ever a thing repugnant to the schoolboard child and its parents; no schoolboard scholar ever deserved punishment. However obvious the fault might seem to a disciplinarian, 'No, I never' exonerated it as something that had not happened. Public schoolboys and private schoolboys of the upper and middle class had their fling and took their thrashings, when they were found out, as a piece of bad luck, but 'our Bert' and 'our Sid' were of those for whom there is no condemnation; if they were punished it was for faults that 'no, they never' committed. Naturally the grown-up generation of Berts and Sids, the voters and householders, do not realise, still less admit, that it was they who called the tune to which the politicians danced. They had to choose between the vote-mongers and the so-called 'scare-mongers,' and their verdict was for the vote-mongers all the time. And now they are bitter; they are being punished, and punishment is not a thing that they have been schooled to bear. The taxes that are falling on them are a grievous source of discontent, and the military service that will be imposed on them, for the first time in their lives, will be another. There is a more lovable side to their character under misfortune, though," added the young clergyman. "Deep down in their hearts there was a very real affection for the old dynasty. Future historians will perhaps be able to explain how and why the Royal Family of Great Britain captured the imaginations of its subjects in so genuine and lasting a fashion. Among the poorest and the most matter-of-fact, for whom the name of no public man, politician or philanthropist, stands out with any especial significance, the old Queen, and the dead King, the dethroned monarch and the young prince live in a sort of domestic Pantheon, a recollection that is a proud and wistful personal possession when so little remains to be proud of or to possess. There is no favour that I am so often asked for among my poorer parishioners as the gift of the picture of this or that member of the old dynasty. 'I have got all of them, only except Princess Mary,' an old woman said to me last week, and she nearly cried with pleasure when I brought her an old Bystander portrait that filled the gap in her collection. And on Queen Alexandra's day they bring out and wear the faded wild-rose favours that they bought with their pennies in days gone by."

"The tragedy of the enactment that is about to enforce military service on these people is that it comes when they've no longer a country to fight for," said Yeovil.

The young clergyman gave an exclamation of bitter impatience.

"That is the cruel mockery of the whole thing. Every now and then in the course of my work I have come across lads who were really drifting to the bad through the good qualities in them. A clean combative strain in their blood, and a natural turn for adventure, made the ordinary anaemic routine of shop or warehouse or factory almost unbearable for them. What splendid little soldiers they would have made, and how grandly the discipline of a military training would have steadied them in after-life when steadiness was wanted. The only adventure that their surroundings offered them has been the adventure of practising mildly criminal misdeeds without getting landed in reformatories and prisons; those of them that have not been successful in keeping clear of detection are walking round and round prison yards, experiencing the operation of a discipline that breaks and does not build. They were merry-hearted boys once, with nothing of the criminal or ne'er-do-weel in their natures, and now—have you ever seen a prison yard, with that walk round and round and round between grey walls under a blue sky?"

Yeovil nodded.

"It's good enough for criminals and imbeciles," said the parson, "but think of it for those boys, who might have been marching along to the tap of the drum, with a laugh on their lips instead of Hell in their hearts. I have had Hell in my heart sometimes, when I have come in touch with cases like those. I suppose you are thinking that I am a strange sort of parson."

"I was just defining you in my mind," said Yeovil, "as a man of God, with an infinite tenderness for little devils."

The clergyman flushed.

"Rather a fine epitaph to have on one's tombstone," he said, "especially if the tombstone were in some crowded city graveyard. I suppose I am a man of God, but I don't think I could be called a man of peace."

Looking at the strong young face, with its suggestion of a fighting prior of bygone days more marked than ever, Yeovil mentally agreed that he could not.

"I have learned one thing in life," continued the young man, "and that is that peace is not for this world. Peace is what God gives us when He takes us into His rest. Beat your sword into a ploughshare if you like, but beat your enemy into smithereens first."

A long-drawn cry, repeated again and again, detached itself from the throb and hoot and whir of the street traffic.

"Speshul! Military service, spesh-ul!"

The young clergyman sprang from his seat and went up the staircase in a succession of bounds, causing the domino players and novelette readers to look up for a moment in mild astonishment. In a few seconds he was back again, with a copy of an afternoon paper. The Imperial Rescript was set forth in heavy type, in parallel columns of English and German. As the young man read a deep burning flush spread over his face, then ebbed away into a chalky whiteness. He read the announcement to the end, then handed the paper to Yeovil, and left without a word.

Beneath the courtly politeness and benignant phraseology of the document ran a trenchant searing irony. The British born subjects of the Germanic Crown, inhabiting the islands of Great Britain and Ireland, had habituated themselves as a people to the disuse of arms, and resolutely excluded military service and national training from their political system and daily life. Their judgment that they were unsuited as a race to bear arms and conform to military discipline was not to be set aside. Their new Overlord did not propose to do violence to their feelings and customs by requiring from them the personal military sacrifices and services which were rendered by his subjects German-born. The British subjects of the Crown were to remain a people consecrated to peaceful pursuits, to commerce and trade and husbandry. The defence of their coasts and shipping and the maintenance of order and general safety would be guaranteed by a garrison of German troops, with the co-operation of the Imperial war fleet. German-born subjects residing temporarily or permanently in the British Isles would come under the same laws respecting compulsory military service as their fellow-subjects of German blood in the other parts of the Empire, and special enactments would be drawn up to ensure that their interests did not suffer from a periodical withdrawal on training or other military calls. Necessarily a heavily differentiated scale of war taxation would fall on British taxpayers, to provide for the upkeep of the garrison and to equalise the services and sacrifices rendered by the two branches of his Majesty's subjects. As military service was not henceforth open to any subject of British birth no further necessity for any training or exercise of a military nature existed, therefore all rifle clubs, drill associations, cadet corps and similar bodies were henceforth declared to be illegal. No weapons other than guns for specified sporting purposes, duly declared and registered and open to inspection when required, could be owned, purchased, or carried. The science of arms was to be eliminated altogether from the life of a people who had shown such marked repugnance to its study and practice.

The cold irony of the measure struck home with the greater force because its nature was so utterly unexpected. Public anticipation had guessed at various forms of military service, aggressively irksome or tactfully lightened as the case might be, in any event certain to be bitterly unpopular, and now there had come this contemptuous boon, which had removed, at one stroke, the bogey of compulsory military service from the troubled imaginings of the British people, and fastened on them the cruel distinction of being in actual fact what an enemy had called them in splenetic scorn long years ago—a nation of shopkeepers. Aye, something even below that level, a race of shopkeepers who were no longer a nation.

Yeovil crumpled the paper in his hand and went out into the sunlit street. A sudden roll of drums and crash of brass music filled the air. A company of Bavarian infantry went by, in all the pomp and circumstance of martial array and the joyous swing of rapid rhythmic movement. The street echoed and throbbed in the Englishman's ears with the exultant pulse of youth and mastery set to loud Pagan music. A group of lads from the tea-shop clustered on the pavement and watched the troops go by, staring at a phase of life in which they had no share. The martial trappings, the swaggering joy of life, the comradeship of camp and barracks, the hard discipline of drill yard and fatigue duty, the long sentry watches, the trench digging, forced marches, wounds, cold, hunger, makeshift hospitals, and the blood-wet laurels—these were not for them. Such things they might only guess at, or see on a cinema film, darkly; they belonged to the civilian nation.

The function of afternoon tea was still being languidly observed in the big drawing-room when Yeovil returned to Berkshire Street. Cicely was playing the part of hostess to a man of perhaps forty-one years of age, who looked slightly older from his palpable attempts to look very much younger. Percival Plarsey was a plump, pale-faced, short-legged individual, with puffy cheeks, over-prominent nose, and thin colourless hair. His mother, with nothing more than maternal prejudice to excuse her, had discovered some twenty odd years ago that he was a well-favoured young man, and had easily imbued her son with the same opinion. The slipping away of years and the natural transition of the unathletic boy into the podgy unhealthy-looking man did little to weaken the tradition; Plarsey had never been able to relinquish the idea that a youthful charm and comeliness still centred in his person, and laboured daily at his toilet with the devotion that a hopelessly lost cause is so often able to inspire. He babbled incessantly about himself and the accessory futilities of his life in short, neat, complacent sentences, and in a voice that Ronald Storre said reminded one of a fat bishop blessing a butter-making competition. While he babbled he kept his eyes fastened on his listeners to observe the impression which his important little announcements and pronouncements were making. On the present occasion he was pattering forth a detailed description of the upholstery and fittings of his new music-room.

"All the hangings, violette de Parme, all the furniture, rosewood. The only ornament in the room is a replica of the Mozart statue in Vienna. Nothing but Mozart is to be played in the room. Absolutely, nothing but Mozart."

"You will get rather tired of that, won't you?" said Cicely, feeling that she was expected to comment on this tremendous announcement.

"One gets tired of everything," said Plarsey, with a fat little sigh of resignation. "I can't tell you how tired I am of Rubenstein, and one day I suppose I shall be tired of Mozart, and violette de Parme and rosewood. I never thought it possible that I could ever tire of jonquils, and now I simply won't have one in the house. Oh, the scene the other day because some one brought some jonquils into the house! I'm afraid I was dreadfully rude, but I really couldn't help it."

He could talk like this through a long summer day or a long winter evening.

Yeovil belonged to a race forbidden to bear arms. At the moment he would gladly have contented himself with the weapons with which nature had endowed him, if he might have kicked and pommelled the abhorrent specimen of male humanity whom he saw before him.

Instead he broke into the conversation with an inspired flash of malicious untruthfulness.

"It is wonderful," he observed carelessly, "how popular that Viennese statue of Mozart has become. A friend who inspects County Council Art Schools tells me you find a copy of it in every class-room you go into."

It was a poor substitute for physical violence, but it was all that civilisation allowed him in the way of relieving his feelings; it had, moreover, the effect of making Plarsey profoundly miserable.

XII

The Travelling Companions

The train bearing Yeovil on his visit to Torywood slid and rattled westward through the hazy dreamland of an English summer landscape. Seen from the train windows the stark bare ugliness of the metalled line was forgotten, and the eye rested only on the green solitude that unfolded itself as the miles went slipping by. Tall grasses and meadow-weeds stood in deep shocks, field after field, between the leafy boundaries of hedge or coppice, thrusting themselves higher and higher till they touched the low sweeping branches of the trees that here and there overshadowed them. Broad streams, bordered with a heavy fringe of reed and sedge, went winding away into a green distance where woodland and meadowland seemed indefinitely prolonged; narrow streamlets, lost to view in the growth that they fostered, disclosed their presence merely by the water-weed that showed in a riband of rank verdure threading the mellower green of the fields. On the stream banks moorhens walked with jerky confident steps, in the easy boldness of those who had a couple of other elements at their disposal in an emergency; more timorous partridges raced away from the apparition of the train, looking all leg and neck, like little forest elves fleeing from human encounter. And in the distance, over the tree line, a heron or two flapped with slow measured wing-beats and an air of being bent on an immeasurably longer journey than the train that hurtled so frantically along the rails. Now and then the meadowland changed itself suddenly into orchard, with close-growing trees already showing the measure of their coming harvest, and then strawyard and farm buildings would slide into view; heavy dairy cattle, roan and skewbald and dappled, stood near the gates, drowsily resentful of insect stings, and bunched-up companies of ducks halted in seeming irresolution between the charms of the horse-pond and the alluring neighbourhood of the farm kitchen. Away by the banks of some rushing mill-stream, in a setting of copse and cornfield, a village might be guessed at, just a hint of red roof, grey wreathed chimney and old church tower as seen from the windows of the passing train, and over it all brooded a happy, settled calm, like the dreaming murmur of a trout-stream and the far-away cawing of rooks.

It was a land where it seemed as if it must be always summer and generally afternoon, a land where bees hummed among the wild thyme and in the flower beds of cottage gardens, where the harvest-mice rustled amid the corn and nettles, and the mill-race flowed cool and silent through water-weeds and dark tunnelled sluices, and made soft droning music with the wooden mill-wheel. And the music carried with it the wording of old undying rhymes, and sang of the jolly, uncaring, uncared-for miller, of the farmer who went riding upon his grey mare, of the mouse who lived beneath the merry mill-pin, of the sweet music on yonder green hill and the dancers all in yellow—the songs and fancies of a lingering olden time, when men took life as children take a long summer day, and went to bed at last with a simple trust in something they could not have explained.

Yeovil watched the passing landscape with the intent hungry eyes of a man who revisits a scene that holds high place in his affections. His imagination raced even quicker than the train, following winding roads and twisting valleys into unseen distances, picturing farms and hamlets, hills and hollows, clattering inn yards and sleepy woodlands.

"A beautiful country," said his only fellow-traveller, who was also gazing at the fleeting landscape; "surely a country worth fighting for."

He spoke in fairly correct English, but he was unmistakably a foreigner; one could have allotted him with some certainty to the Eastern half of Europe.

"A beautiful country, as you say," replied Yeovil; then he added the question, "Are you German?"

"No, Hungarian," said the other; "and you, you are English?" he asked.

"I have been much in England, but I am from Russia," said Yeovil, purposely misleading his companion on the subject of his nationality in order to induce him to talk with greater freedom on a delicate topic. While living among foreigners in a foreign land he had shrunk from hearing his country's disaster discussed, or even alluded to; now he was anxious to learn what unprejudiced foreigners thought of the catastrophe and the causes which had led up to it.

"It is a strange spectacle, a wonder, is it not so?" resumed the other, "a great nation such as this was, one of the greatest nations in modern times, or of any time, carrying its flag and its language into all parts of the world, and now, after one short campaign, it is—"

And he shrugged his shoulders many times and made clucking noises at the roof of his voice, like a hen calling to a brood of roving chickens.

"They grew soft," he resumed; "great world-commerce brings great luxury, and luxury brings softness. They had everything to warn them, things happening in their own time and before their eyes, and they would not be warned. They had seen, in one generation, the rise of the military and naval power of the Japanese, a brown-skinned race living in some island rice fields in a tropical sea, a people one thought of in connection with paper fans and flowers and pretty tea-gardens, who suddenly marched and sailed into the world's gaze as a Great Power; they had seen, too, the rise of the Bulgars, a poor herd of zaptieh-ridden peasants, with a few students scattered in exile in Bukarest and Odessa, who shot up in one generation to be an armed and aggressive nation with history in its hands. The English saw these things happening around them, and with a war-cloud growing blacker and bigger and always more threatening on their own threshold they sat down to grow soft and peaceful. They grew soft and accommodating in all things in religion—"

"In religion?" said Yeovil.

"In religion, yes," said his companion emphatically; "they had come to look on the Christ as a sort of amiable elder Brother, whose letters from abroad were worth reading. Then, when they had emptied all the divine mystery and wonder out of their faith naturally they grew tired of it, oh, but dreadfully tired of it. I know many English of the country parts, and always they tell me they go to church once in each week to set the good example to the servants. They were tired of their faith, but they were not virile enough to become real Pagans; their dancing fauns were good young men who tripped Morris dances and ate health foods and believed in a sort of Socialism which made for the greatest dulness of the greatest number. You will find plenty of them still if you go into what remains of social London."

Yeovil gave a grunt of acquiescence.

"They grew soft in their political ideas," continued the unsparing critic; "for the old insular belief that all foreigners were devils and rogues they substituted another belief, equally grounded on insular lack of knowledge, that most foreigners were amiable, good fellows, who only needed to be talked to and patted on the back to become your friends and benefactors. They began to believe that a foreign

Minister would relinquish long-cherished schemes of national policy and hostile expansion if he came over on a holiday and was asked down to country houses and shown the tennis court and the rock-garden and the younger children. Listen. I once heard it solemnly stated at an after-dinner debate in some literary club that a certain very prominent German statesman had a daughter at school in England, and that future friendly relations between the two countries were improved in prospect, if not assured, by that circumstance. You think I am laughing; I am recording a fact, and the men present were politicians and statesmen as well as literary dilettanti. It was an insular lack of insight that worked the mischief, or some of the mischief. We, in Hungary, we live too much cheek by jowl with our racial neighbours to have many illusions about them. Austrians, Roumanians, Serbs, Italians, Czechs, we know what they think of us, and we know what to think of them, we know what we want in the world, and we know what they want; that knowledge does not send us flying at each other's throats, but it does keep us from growing soft. Ah, the British lion was in a hurry to inaugurate the Millennium and to lie down gracefully with the lamb. He made two mistakes, only two, but they were very bad ones; the Millennium hadn't arrived, and it was not a lamb that he was lying down with."

"You do not like the English, I gather," said Yeovil, as the Hungarian went off into a short burst of satirical laughter.

"I have always liked them," he answered, "but now I am angry with them for being soft. Here is my station," he added, as the train slowed down, and he commenced to gather his belongings together. "I am angry with them," he continued, as a final word on the subject, "because I hate the Germans."

He raised his hat punctiliously in a parting salute and stepped out on to the platform. His place was taken by a large, loose-limbed man, with florid face and big staring eyes, and an immense array of fishing-basket, rod, fly-cases, and so forth. He was of the type that one could instinctively locate as a loud-voiced, self-constituted authority on whatever topic might happen to be discussed in the bars of small hotels.

"Are you English?" he asked, after a preliminary stare at Yeovil.

This time Yeovil did not trouble to disguise his nationality; he nodded curtly to his questioner.

"Glad of that," said the fisherman; "I don't like travelling with Germans."

"Unfortunately," said Yeovil, "we have to travel with them, as partners in the same State concern, and not by any means the predominant partner either."

"Oh, that will soon right itself," said the other with loud assertiveness, "that will right itself damn soon."

"Nothing in politics rights itself," said Yeovil; "things have to be righted, which is a different matter."

"What d'y'mean?" said the fisherman, who did not like to have his assertions taken up and shaken into shape.

"We have given a clever and domineering people a chance to plant themselves down as masters in our land; I don't imagine that they are going to give us an easy chance to push them out. To do that we shall have to be a little cleverer than they are, a little harder, a little fiercer, and a good deal more self-sacrificing than we have been in my lifetime or in yours."

"We'll be that, right enough," said the fisherman; "we mean business this time. The last war wasn't a war, it was a snap. We weren't prepared and they were. That won't happen again, bless you. I know what I'm talking about. I go up and down the country, and I hear what people are saying."

Yeovil privately doubted if he ever heard anything but his own opinions.

"It stands to reason," continued the fisherman, "that a highly civilised race like ours, with the record that we've had for leading the whole world, is not going to be held under for long by a lot of damned sausage-eating Germans. Don't you believe it! I know what I'm talking about. I've travelled about the world a bit."

Yeovil shrewdly suspected that the world travels amounted to nothing more than a trip to the United States and perhaps the Channel Islands, with, possibly, a week or fortnight in Paris.

"It isn't the past we've got to think of, it's the future," said Yeovil. "Other maritime Powers had pasts to look back on; Spain and Holland, for instance. The past didn't help them when they let their sea-sovereignty slip from them. That is a matter of history and not very distant history either."

"Ah, that's where you make a mistake," said the other; "our sea-sovereignty hasn't slipped from us, and won't do, neither. There's the British Empire beyond the seas; Canada, Australia, New Zealand, East Africa."

He rolled the names round his tongue with obvious relish.

"If it was a list of first-class battleships, and armoured cruisers and destroyers and airships that you were reeling off, there would be some comfort and hope in the situation," said Yeovil; "the loyalty of the colonies is a splendid thing, but it is only pathetically splendid because it can do so little to recover for us what we've lost. Against the Zeppelin air fleet, and the Dreadnought sea squadrons and the new Gelberhaus cruisers, the last word in maritime mobility, of what avail is loyal devotion plus half-a-dozen warships, one keel to ten, scattered over one or two ocean coasts?"

"Ah, but they'll build," said the fisherman confidently; "they'll build. They're only waiting to enlarge their dockyard accommodation and get the right class of artificers and engineers and workmen together. The money will be forthcoming somehow, and they'll start in and build."

"And do you suppose," asked Yeovil in slow bitter contempt, "that the victorious nation is going to sit and watch and wait till the defeated foe has created a new war fleet, big enough to drive it from the seas? Do you suppose it is going to watch keel added to keel, gun to gun, airship to airship, till its preponderance has been wiped out or even threatened? That sort of thing is done once in a generation, not twice. Who is going to protect Australia or New Zealand while they enlarge their dockyards and hangars and build their dreadnoughts and their airships?"

"Here's my station and I'm not sorry," said the fisherman, gathering his tackle together and rising to depart; "I've listened to you long enough. You and me wouldn't agree, not if we was to talk all day. Fact is, I'm an out-and-out patriot and you're only a half-hearted one. That's what you are, half-hearted."

And with that parting shot he left the carriage and lounged heavily down the platform, a patriot who had never handled a rifle or mounted a horse or pulled an oar, but who had never flinched from demolishing his country's enemies with his tongue.

"England has never had any lack of patriots of that type," thought Yeovil sadly; "so many patriots and so little patriotism."

XIII

Torywood

Yeovil got out of the train at a small, clean, wayside station, and rapidly formed the conclusion that neatness, abundant leisure, and a devotion to the cultivation of wallflowers and wyandottes were the prevailing influences of the station-master's life. The train slid away into the hazy distance of trees and meadows, and left the traveller standing in a world that seemed to be made up in equal parts of rock garden, chicken coops, and whiskey advertisements. The station-master, who appeared also to act as emergency porter, took Yeovil's ticket with the gesture of a kind-hearted person brushing away a troublesome wasp, and returned to a study of the Poultry Chronicle, which was giving its readers sage counsel concerning the ailments of belated July chickens. Yeovil called to mind the station-master of a tiny railway town in Siberia, who had held him in long and rather intelligent converse on the poetical merits and demerits of Shelley, and he wondered what the result would be if he were to engage the English official in a discussion on Lermontoff—or for the matter of that, on Shelley. The temptation to experiment was, however, removed by the arrival of a young groom, with brown eyes and a friendly smile, who hurried into the station and took Yeovil once more into a world where he was of fleeting importance.

In the roadway outside was a four-wheeled dogcart with a pair of the famous Torywood blue roans. It was an agreeable variation in modern locomotion to be met at a station with high-class horseflesh instead of the ubiquitous motor, and the landscape was not of such a nature that one wished to be whirled through it in a cloud of dust. After a quick spin of some ten or fifteen minutes through twisting hedge-girt country roads, the roans turned in at a wide gateway, and went with dancing, rhythmic step along the park drive. The screen of oak-crowned upland suddenly fell away and a grey sharp-cornered building came into view in a setting of low growing beeches and dark pines. Torywood was not a stately, reposeful-looking house; it lay amid the sleepy landscape like a couched watchdog with pricked ears and wakeful eyes. Built somewhere about the last years of Dutch William's reign, it had been a centre, ever since, for the political life of the countryside; a storm centre of discontent or a rallying ground for the well affected, as the circumstances of the day might entail. On the stone-flagged terrace in front of the house, with its quaint leaden figures of Diana pursuing a hound-pressed stag, successive squires and lords of Torywood had walked to and fro with their friends, watching the thunderclouds on the political horizon or the shifting shadows on the sundial of political favour, tapping the political barometer for indications of change, working out a party campaign or arranging for the support of some national movement. To and fro they had gone in their respective generations, men with the passion for statecraft and political combat strong in their veins, and many oft-recurring names had echoed under those wakeful-looking casements, names spoken in anger or exultation, or murmured in fear and anxiety: Bolingbroke, Charles Edward, Walpole, the Farmer King, Bonaparte, Pitt, Wellington, Peel, Gladstone—echo and Time might have graven those names on the stone flags and grey walls. And now one tired old woman walked there, with names on her lips that she never uttered.

A friendly riot of fox terriers and spaniels greeted the carriage, leaping and rolling and yelping in an exuberance of sociability, as though horses and coachman and groom were comrades who had been absent for long months instead of half an hour. An indiscriminately affectionate puppy lay flat and whimpering at Yeovil's feet, sending up little showers of gravel with its wildly thumping tail, while two of the terriers raced each other madly across lawn and shrubbery, as though to show the blue roans what speed really was. The laughing-eyed young groom disentangled the puppy from between Yeovil's legs, and then he was ushered into the grey silence of the entrance hall, leaving sunlight and noise and the stir of life behind him.

"Her ladyship will see you in her writing room," he was told, and he followed a servant along the dark passages to the well-remembered room.

There was something tragic in the sudden contrast between the vigour and youth and pride of life that Yeovil had seen crystallised in those dancing, high-stepping horses, scampering dogs, and alert, clean-limbed young men-servants, and the age-frail woman who came forward to meet him.

Eleanor, Dowager Lady Greymarten, had for more than half a century been the ruling spirit at Torywood. The affairs of the county had not sufficed for her untiring activities of mind and body; in the wider field of national and Imperial service she had worked and schemed and fought with an energy and a far-sightedness that came probably from the blend of caution and bold restlessness in her Scottish blood. For many educated minds the arena of politics and public life is a weariness of dust and disgust, to others it is a fascinating study, to be watched from the comfortable seat of a spectator. To her it was a home. In her town house or down at Torywood, with her writing-pad on her knee and the telephone at her elbow, or in personal counsel with some trusted colleague or persuasive argument with a halting adherent or half-convinced opponent, she had laboured on behalf of the poor and the ill-equipped, had fought for her idea of the Right, and above all, for the safety and sanity of her Fatherland. Spadework when necessary and leadership when called for, came alike within the scope of her activities, and not least of her achievements, though perhaps she hardly realised it, was the force of her example, a lone, indomitable fighter calling to the half-caring and the half-discouraged, to the laggard and the slow-moving.

And now she came across the room with "the tired step of a tired king," and that look which the French so expressively called l'air defait. The charm which Heaven bestows on old ladies, reserving its highest gift to the end, had always seemed in her case to be lost sight of in the dignity and interest of a great dame who was still in the full prime of her fighting and ruling powers. Now, in Yeovil's eyes, she had suddenly come to be very old, stricken with the forlorn languor of one who knows that death will be weary to wait for. She had spared herself nothing in the long labour, the ceaseless building, the watch and ward, and in one short autumn week she had seen the overthrow of all that she had built, the falling asunder of the world in which she had laboured. Her life's end was like a harvest home when blight and storm have laid waste the fruit of long toil and unsparing outlay. Victory had been her goal, the death or victory of old heroic challenge, for she had always dreamed to die fighting to the last; death or victory—and the gods had given her neither, only the bitterness of a defeat that could not be measured in words, and the weariness of a life that had outlived happiness or hope. Such was Eleanor, Dowager Lady Greymarten, a shadow amid the young red-blooded life at Torywood, but a shadow that was too real to die, a shadow that was stronger than the substance that surrounded it.

Yeovil talked long and hurriedly of his late travels, of the vast Siberian forests and rivers, the desolate tundras, the lakes and marshes where the wild swans rear their broods, the flower carpet of the summer fields and the winter ice-mantle of Russia's northern sea. He talked as a man talks who avoids the subject that is uppermost in his mind, and in the mind of his hearer, as one who looks away from a wound or deformity that is too cruel to be taken notice of.

Tea was served in a long oak-panelled gallery, where generations of Mustelfords had romped and played as children, and remained yet in effigy, in a collection of more or less faithful portraits. After tea Yeovil was taken by his hostess to the aviaries, which constituted the sole claim which Torywood possessed to being considered a show place. The third Earl of Greymarten had collected rare and interesting birds, somewhere about the time when Gilbert White was penning the last of his deathless letters, and his successors in the title had perpetuated the hobby. Little lawns and ponds and shrubberies were partitioned off for the various ground-loving species, and higher cages with interlacing perches and rockwork shelves accommodated the birds whose natural expression of movement was on the wing. Quails and francolins scurried about under low-growing shrubs, peacock-pheasants strutted and sunned themselves, pugnacious ruffs engaged in perfunctory battles, from force of habit now that the rivalry of the mating season was over; choughs, ravens, and loud-throated gulls occupied sections of a vast rockery, and bright-hued Chinese pond-herons and delicately stepping egrets waded among the waterlilies of a marble-terraced tank. One or two dusky shapes seen dimly in the recesses of a large cage built round a hollow tree would be lively owls when evening came on.

In the course of his many wanderings Yeovil had himself contributed three or four inhabitants to this little feathered town, and he went round the enclosures, renewing old acquaintances and examining new additions.

"The falcon cage is empty," said Lady Greymarten, pointing to a large wired dome that towered high above the other enclosures, "I let the lanner fly free one day. The other birds may be reconciled to their comfortable quarters and abundant food and absence of dangers, but I don't think all those things could make up to a falcon for the wild range of cliff and desert. When one has lost one's own liberty one feels a quicker sympathy for other caged things, I suppose."

There was silence for a moment, and then the Dowager went on, in a wistful, passionate voice:

"I am an old woman now, Murrey, I must die in my cage. I haven't the strength to fight. Age is a very real and very cruel thing, though we may shut our eyes to it and pretend it is not there. I thought at one time that I should never really know what it meant, what it brought to one. I thought of it as a messenger that one could keep waiting out in the yard till the very last moment. I know now what it means. . . But you, Murrey, you are young, you can fight. Are you going to be a fighter, or the very humble servant of the fait accompli?"

"I shall never be the servant of the fait accompli," said Yeovil. "I loathe it. As to fighting, one must first find out what weapon to use, and how to use it effectively. One must watch and wait."

"One must not wait too long," said the old woman. "Time is on their side, not ours. It is the young people we must fight for now, if they are ever to fight for us. A new generation will spring up, a weaker memory of old glories will survive, the eclat of the ruling race will capture young imaginations. If I had your youth, Murrey, and your sex, I would become a commercial traveller."

"A commercial traveller!" exclaimed Yeovil.

"Yes, one whose business took him up and down the country, into contact with all classes, into homes and shops and inns and railway carriages. And as I travelled I would work, work on the minds of every boy and girl I came across, every young father and young mother too, every young couple that were going to be man and wife. I would awaken or keep alive in their memory the things that we have been, the grand, brave things that some of our race have done, and I would stir up a longing, a determination for the future that we must win back. I would be a counter-agent to the agents of the fait accompli. In course of time the Government would find out what I was doing, and I should be sent out of the country, but I should have accomplished something, and others would carry on the work. That is what I would do. Murrey, even if it is to be a losing battle, fight it, fight it!"

Yeovil knew that the old lady was fighting her last battle, rallying the discouraged, and spurring on the backward.

A footman came to announce that the carriage waited to take him back to the station. His hostess walked with him through the hall, and came out on to the stone-flagged terrace, the terrace from which a former Lady Greymarten had watched the twinkling bonfires that told of Waterloo.

Yeovil said good-bye to her as she stood there, a wan, shrunken shadow, yet with a greater strength and reality in her flickering life than those parrot men and women that fluttered and chattered through London drawing-rooms and theatre foyers.

As the carriage swung round a bend in the drive Yeovil looked back at Torywood, a lone, grey building, couched like a watchdog with pricked ears and wakeful eyes in the midst of the sleeping landscape. An old pleading voice was still ringing in his ears:

> *Imperious and yet forlorn,*
> *Came through the silence of the trees,*
> *The echoes of a golden horn,*
> *Calling to distances.*

Somehow Yeovil knew that he would never hear that voice again, and he knew, too, that he would hear it always, with its message, "Be a fighter." And he knew now, with a shamefaced consciousness that sprang suddenly into existence, that the summons would sound for him in vain.

The weary brain-torturing months of fever had left their trail behind, a lassitude of spirit and a sluggishness of blood, a quenching of the desire to roam and court adventure and hardship. In the hours of waking and depression between the raging intervals of delirium he had speculated, with a sort of detached, listless indifference, on the chances of his getting back to life and strength and energy. The prospect of filling a corner of some lonely Siberian graveyard or Finnish cemetery had seemed near realisation at times, and for a man who was already half dead the other half didn't particularly matter. But when he had allowed himself to dwell on the more hopeful side of the case it had always been a complete recovery that awaited him; the same Yeovil as of yore, a little thinner and more lined about the eyes perhaps, would go through life in the same way, alert, resolute, enterprising, ready to start off at short notice for some desert or upland where the eagles were circling and the wild-fowl were calling. He had not reckoned that Death, evaded and held off by the doctors' skill, might exact a compromise, and that only part of the man would go free to the West.

And now he began to realise how little of mental and physical energy he could count on. His own country had never seemed in his eyes so comfort-yielding and to-be-desired as it did now when it had passed into alien keeping and become a prison land as much as a homeland. London with its thin mockery of a Season, and its chattering horde of empty-hearted self-seekers, held no attraction for him, but the spell of English country life was weaving itself round him, now that the charm of the desert was receding into a mist of memories. The waning of pleasant autumn days in an English woodland, the whir of game birds in the clean harvested fields, the grey moist mornings in the saddle, with the magical cry of hounds coming up from some misty hollow, and then the delicious abandon of physical weariness in bathroom and bedroom after a long run, and the heavenly snatched hour of luxurious sleep, before stirring back to life and hunger, the coming of the dinner hour and the jollity of a well-chosen house-party.

That was the call which was competing with that other trumpet-call, and Yeovil knew on which side his choice would incline.

XIV

"A Perfectly Glorious Afternoon"

It was one of the last days of July, cooled and freshened by a touch of rain and dropping back again to a languorous warmth. London looked at its summer best, rain-washed and sun-lit, with the maximum of coming and going in its more fashionable streets.

Cicely Yeovil sat in a screened alcove of the Anchorage Restaurant, a feeding-ground which had lately sprung into favour. Opposite her sat Ronnie, confronting the ruins of what had been a dish of prawns in aspic. Cool and clean and fresh-coloured, he was good to look on in the eyes of his companion, and yet, perhaps, there was a ruffle in her soul that called for some answering disturbance on the part of that superbly tranquil young man, and certainly called in vain. Cicely had set up for herself a fetish of onyx with eyes of jade, and doubtless hungered at times with an unreasonable but perfectly natural hunger for something of flesh and blood. It was the religion of her life to know exactly what she wanted and to see that she got it, but there was no possible guarantee against her occasionally experiencing a desire for something else. It is the golden rule of all religions that no one should really live up to their precepts; when a man observes the principles of his religion too exactly he is in immediate danger of founding a new sect.

"Today is going to be your day of triumph," said Cicely to the young man, who was wondering at the moment whether he would care to embark on an artichoke; "I believe I'm more nervous than you are," she added, "and yet I rather hate the idea of you scoring a great success."

"Why?" asked Ronnie, diverting his mind for a moment from the artichoke question and its ramifications of sauce hollandaise or vinaigre.

"I like you as you are," said Cicely, "just a nice-looking boy to flatter and spoil and pretend to be fond of. You've got a charming young body and you've no soul, and that's such a fascinating combination. If you had a soul you would either dislike or worship me, and I'd much rather have things as they are. And now you are going to go a step beyond that, and other people will applaud you and say that you are wonderful, and invite you to eat with them and motor with them and yacht with them. As soon as that begins to happen, Ronnie, a lot of other things will come to an end. Of course I've always known that you don't really care for me, but as soon as the world knows it you are irrevocably damaged as a plaything. That is the great secret that binds us together, the knowledge that we have no real affection for one another. And this afternoon every one will know that you are a great artist, and no great artist was ever a great lover."

"I shan't be difficult to replace, anyway," said Ronnie, with what he imagined was a becoming modesty; "there are lots of boys standing round ready to be fed and flattered and put on an imaginary pedestal, most of them more or less good-looking and well turned out and amusing to talk to."

"Oh, I dare say I could find a successor for your vacated niche," said Cicely lightly; "one thing I'm determined on though, he shan't be a musician. It's so unsatisfactory to have to share a grand passion with a grand piano. He shall be a delightful young barbarian who would think Saint Saens was a Derby winner or a claret."

"Don't be in too much of a hurry to replace me," said Ronnie, who did not care to have his successor too seriously discussed. "I may not score the success you expect this afternoon."

"My dear boy, a minor crowned head from across the sea is coming to hear you play, and that alone will count as a success with most of your listeners. Also, I've secured a real Duchess for you, which is rather an achievement in the London of today."

"An English Duchess?" asked Ronnie, who had early in life learned to apply the Merchandise Marks Act to ducal titles.

"English, oh certainly, at least as far as the title goes; she was born under the constellation of the Star-spangled Banner. I don't suppose the Duke approves of her being here, lending her countenance to the fait accompli, but when you've got republican blood in your veins a Kaiser is quite as attractive a lodestar as a King, rather more so. And Canon Mousepace is coming," continued Cicely, referring to a closely-written list of guests; "the excellent von Tolb has been attending his church lately, and the Canon is longing to meet her. She is just the sort of person he adores. I fancy he sincerely realises how difficult it will be for the rich to enter the Kingdom of Heaven, and he tries to make up for it by being as nice as possible to them in this world."

Ronnie held out his hand for the list.

"I think you know most of the others," said Cicely, passing it to him.

"Leutnant von Gabelroth?" read out Ronnie; "who is he?"

"In one of the hussar regiments quartered here; a friend of the Grafin's. Ugly but amiable, and I'm told a good cross-country rider. I suppose Murrey will be disgusted at meeting the 'outward and visible sign' under his roof, but these encounters are inevitable as long as he is in London."

"I didn't know Murrey was coming," said Ronnie.

"I believe he's going to look in on us," said Cicely; "it's just as well, you know, otherwise we should have Joan asking in her loudest voice when he was going to be back in England again. I haven't asked her, but she overheard the Grafin arranging to come and hear you play, and I fancy that will be quite enough."

"How about some Turkish coffee?" said Ronnie, who had decided against the artichoke.

"Turkish coffee, certainly, and a cigarette, and a moment's peace before the serious business of the afternoon claims us. Talking about peace, do you know, Ronnie, it has just occurred to me that we have left out one of the most important things in our affaire; we have never had a quarrel."

"I hate quarrels," said Ronnie, "they are so domesticated."

"That's the first time I've ever heard you talk about your home," said Cicely.

"I fancy it would apply to most homes," said Ronnie.

"The last boy-friend I had used to quarrel furiously with me at least once a week," said Cicely reflectively; "but then he had dark slumberous eyes that lit up magnificently when he was angry, so it would have been a sheer waste of God's good gifts not to have sent him into a passion now and then."

"With your excursions into the past and the future you are making me feel dreadfully like an instalment of a serial novel," protested Ronnie; "we have now got to 'synopsis of earlier chapters.'"

"It shan't be teased," said Cicely; "we will live in the present and go no further into the future than to make arrangements for Tuesday's dinner-party. I've asked the Duchess; she would never have forgiven me if she'd found out that I had a crowned head dining with me and hadn't asked her to meet him."

A SUDDEN HUSH DESCENDED ON the company gathered in the great drawing-room at Berkshire Street as Ronnie took his seat at the piano; the voice of Canon Mousepace outlasted the others for a moment or so, and then subsided into a regretful but gracious silence. For the next nine or ten minutes Ronnie held possession of the crowded room, a tense slender figure, with cold green eyes aflame in a sudden fire, and smooth burnished head bent low over the keyboard that yielded a disciplined riot of melody under his strong deft fingers. The world-weary Landgraf forgot for the moment the regrettable trend of his subjects towards Parliamentary Socialism, the excellent Grafin von Tolb forgot all that the Canon had been saying to her for the last ten minutes, forgot the depressing certainty that he would have a great deal more that he wanted to say in the immediate future, over and above the thirty-five minutes or so of discourse that she would contract to listen to next Sunday. And Cicely listened with the wistful equivocal triumph of one whose goose has turned out to be a swan and who realises with secret concern that she has only planned the role of goosegirl for herself.

The last chords died away, the fire faded out of the jade-coloured eyes, and Ronnie became once more a well-groomed youth in a drawing-room full of well-dressed people. But around him rose an explosive clamour of applause and congratulation, the sincere tribute of appreciation and the equally hearty expression of imitative homage.

"It is a great gift, a great gift," chanted Canon Mousepace, "You must put it to a great use. A talent is vouchsafed to us for a purpose; you must fulfil the purpose. Talent such as yours is a responsibility; you must meet that responsibility."

The dictionary of the English language was an inexhaustible quarry, from which the Canon had hewn and fashioned for himself a great reputation.

"You must gom and blay to me at Schlachsenberg," said the kindly-faced Landgraf, whom the world adored and thwarted in about equal proportions. "At Christmas, yes, that will be a good time. We still keep the Christ-Fest at Schlachsenberg, though the 'Sozi' keep telling our schoolchildren that it is only a Christ myth. Never mind, I will have the Vice-President of our Landtag to listen to you; he is 'Sozi' but we are good friends outside the Parliament House; you shall blay to him, my young friendt, and gonfince him that there is a Got in Heaven. You will gom? Yes?"

"It was beautiful," said the Grafin simply; "it made me cry. Go back to the piano again, please, at once."

Perhaps the near neighbourhood of the Canon inspired this command, but the Grafin had been genuinely charmed. She adored good music and she was unaffectedly fond of good-looking boys.

Ronnie went back to the piano and tasted the matured pleasure of a repeated success. Any measure of nervousness that he may have felt at first had completely passed away. He was sure of his audience and he played as though they did not exist. A renewed clamour of excited approval attended the conclusion of his performance.

"It is a triumph, a perfectly glorious triumph," exclaimed the Duchess of Dreyshire, turning to Yeovil, who sat silent among his wife's guests; "isn't it just glorious?" she demanded, with a heavy insistent intonation of the word.

"Is it?" said Yeovil.

"Well, isn't it?" she cried, with a rising inflection, "isn't it just perfectly glorious?"

"I don't know," confessed Yeovil; "you see glory hasn't come very much my way lately." Then, before he exactly realised what he was doing, he raised his voice and quoted loudly for the benefit of half the room:

> *"'Other Romans shall arise,*
> *Heedless of a soldier's name,*
> *Sounds, not deeds, shall win the prize,*
> *Harmony the path to fame.'"*

There was a sort of shiver of surprised silence at Yeovil's end of the room.

"Hell!"

The word rang out in a strong young voice.

"Hell! And it's true, that's the worst of it. It's damned true!"

Yeovil turned, with some dozen others, to see who was responsible for this vigorously expressed statement.

Tony Luton confronted him, an angry scowl on his face, a blaze in his heavy-lidded eyes. The boy was without a conscience, almost without a soul, as priests and parsons reckon souls, but there was a slumbering devil-god within him, and Yeovil's taunting words had broken the slumber. Life had been for Tony a hard school, in which right and wrong, high endeavour and good resolve, were untaught subjects; but there was a sterling something in him, just that something that helped poor street-scavenged men to die brave-fronted deaths in the trenches of Salamanca, that fired a handful of apprentice boys to shut the gates of Derry and stare unflinchingly at grim leaguer and starvation. It was just that nameless something that was lacking in the young musician, who stood at the further end of the room, bathed in a flood of compliment and congratulation, enjoying the honey-drops of his triumph.

Luton pushed his way through the crowd and left the room, without troubling to take leave of his hostess.

"What a strange young man," exclaimed the Duchess; "now do take me into the next room," she went on almost in the same breath, "I'm just dying for some iced coffee."

Yeovil escorted her through the throng of Ronnie-worshippers to the desired haven of refreshment.

"Marvellous!" Mrs. Menteith-Mendlesohnn was exclaiming in ringing trumpet tones; "of course I always knew he could play, but this is not mere piano playing, it is tone-mastery, it is sound magic. Mrs. Yeovil has introduced us to a new star in the musical firmament. Do you know, I feel this afternoon just like Cortez, in the poem, gazing at the newly discovered sea."

"'Silent upon a peak in Darien,'" quoted a penetrating voice that could only belong to Joan Mardle; "I say, can any one picture Mrs. Menteith-Mendlesohnn silent on any peak or under any circumstances?"

If any one had that measure of imagination, no one acknowledged the fact.

"A great gift and a great responsibility," Canon Mousepace was assuring the Grafin; "the power of evoking sublime melody is akin to the power of awakening thought; a musician can appeal to dormant consciousness as the preacher can appeal to dormant conscience. It is a responsibility, an instrument for good or evil. Our young friend here, we may be sure, will use it as an instrument for good. He has, I feel certain, a sense of his responsibility."

"He is a nice boy," said the Grafin simply; "he has such pretty hair."

In one of the window recesses Rhapsodie Pantril was talking vaguely but beautifully to a small audience on the subject of chromatic chords; she had the advantage of knowing what she was talking about, an advantage that her listeners did not in the least share. "All through his playing there ran a tone-note of malachite green," she declared recklessly, feeling safe from immediate contradiction; "malachite green, my colour—the colour of striving."

Having satisfied the ruling passion that demanded gentle and dextrous self-advertisement, she realised that the Augusta Smith in her craved refreshment, and moved with one of her over-awed admirers towards the haven where peaches and iced coffee might be considered a certainty.

The refreshment alcove, which was really a good-sized room, a sort of chapel-of-ease to the larger drawing-room, was already packed with a crowd who felt that they could best discuss Ronnie's triumph between mouthfuls of fruit salad and iced draughts of hock-cup. So brief is human glory that two or three independent souls had even now drifted from the theme of the moment on to other more personally interesting topics.

"Iced mulberry salad, my dear, it's a specialite de la maison, so to speak; they say the roving husband brought the recipe from Astrakhan, or Seville, or some such outlandish place."

"I wish my husband would roam about a bit and bring back strange palatable dishes. No such luck, he's got asthma and has to keep on a gravel soil with a south aspect and all sorts of other restrictions."

"I don't think you're to be pitied in the least; a husband with asthma is like a captive golf-ball, you can always put your hand on him when you want him."

"All the hangings, violette de Parme, all the furniture, rosewood. Nothing is to be played in it except Mozart. Mozart only. Some of my friends wanted me to have a replica of the Mozart statue at Vienna put up in a corner of the room, with flowers always around it, but I really couldn't. I couldn't. One is so tired of it, one sees it everywhere. I couldn't do it. I'm like that, you know."

"Yes, I've secured the hero of the hour, Ronnie Storre, oh yes, rather. He's going to join our yachting trip, third week of August. We're going as far afield as Fiume, in the Adriatic—or is it the AEgean? Won't it be jolly. Oh no, we're not asking Mrs. Yeovil; it's quite a small yacht you know—at least, it's a small party."

The excellent von Tolb took her departure, bearing off with her the Landgraf, who had already settled the date and duration of Ronnie's Christmas visit.

"It will be dull, you know," he warned the prospective guest; "our Landtag will not be sitting, and what is a bear-garden without the bears? However, we haf some wildt schwein in our woods, we can show you some sport in that way."

Ronnie instantly saw himself in a well-fitting shooting costume, with a Tyrolese hat placed at a very careful angle on his head, but he confessed that the other details of boar-hunting were rather beyond him.

With the departure of the von Tolb party Canon Mousepace gravitated decently but persistently towards a corner where the Duchess, still at concert pitch, was alternatively praising Ronnie's performance and the mulberry salad. Joan Mardle, who formed one of the group, was not openly praising any one, but she was paying a silent tribute to the salad.

"We were just talking about Ronnie Storre's music, Canon," said the Duchess; "I consider it just perfectly glorious."

"It's a great talent, isn't it, Canon," put in Joan briskly, "and of course it's a responsibility as well, don't you think? Music can be such an influence, just as eloquence can; don't you agree with me?"

The quarry of the English language was of course a public property, but it was disconcerting to have one's own particular barrow-load of sentence-building material carried off before one's eyes. The Canon's impressive homily on Ronnie's gift and its possibilities had to be hastily whittled down to a weakly acquiescent, "Quite so, quite so."

"Have you tasted this iced mulberry salad, Canon?" asked the Duchess; "it's perfectly luscious. Just hurry along and get some before it's all gone."

And her Grace hurried along in an opposite direction, to thank Cicely for past favours and to express lively gratitude for the Tuesday to come.

The guests departed, with a rather irritating slowness, for which perhaps the excellence of Cicely's buffet arrangements was partly responsible. The great drawing-room seemed to grow larger and more oppressive as the human wave receded, and the hostess fled at last with some relief to the narrower limits of her writing-room and the sedative influences of a cigarette. She was inclined to be sorry for herself; the triumph of the afternoon had turned out much as she had predicted at lunch time. Her idol of onyx had not been swept from its pedestal, but the pedestal itself had an air of being packed up ready for transport to some other temple. Ronnie would be flattered and spoiled by half a hundred people, just because he could conjure sounds out of a keyboard, and Cicely felt no great incentive to go on flattering and spoiling him herself. And Ronnie would acquiesce in his dismissal with the good grace born of indifference—the surest guarantor of perfect manners. Already he had social engagements for the coming months in which she had no share; the drifting apart would be mutual. He had been an intelligent and amusing companion, and he had played the game as she had wished it to be played, without the fatigue of keeping up pretences which neither of them could have believed in. "Let us have a wonderfully good time together" had been the single stipulation in their unwritten treaty of comradeship, and they had had the good time. Their whole-hearted pursuit of material happiness would go on as keenly as before, but they would hunt in different company, that was all. Yes, that was all. . .

Cicely found the effect of her cigarette less sedative than she was disposed to exact. It might be necessary to change the brand. Some ten or eleven days later Yeovil read an announcement in the papers that, in spite of handsome offers of increased salary, Mr. Tony Luton, the original singer of the popular ditty "Eccleston Square," had terminated his engagement with Messrs. Isaac Grosvenor and Leon Hebhardt of the Caravansery Theatre, and signed on as a deck hand in the Canadian Marine.

Perhaps after all there had been some shred of glory amid the trumpet triumph of that July afternoon.

XV

The Intelligent Anticipator of Wants

Two of Yeovil's London clubs, the two that he had been accustomed to frequent, had closed their doors after the catastrophe. One of them had perished from off the face of the earth, its fittings had been sold and its papers lay stored in some solicitor's office, a tit-bit of material for the pen of some future historian. The other had transplanted itself to Delhi, whither it had removed its early Georgian furniture and its traditions, and sought to reproduce its St. James's Street atmosphere as nearly as the conditions of a tropical Asiatic city would permit. There remained the Cartwheel, a considerably newer institution, which had sprung into existence somewhere about the time of Yeovil's last sojourn in England; he had joined it on the solicitation of a friend who was interested in the venture, and his bankers had paid his subscription during his absence. As he had never been inside its doors there could be no depressing comparisons to make between its present state and aforetime glories, and Yeovil turned into its portals one afternoon with the adventurous detachment of a man who breaks new ground and challenges new experiences.

He entered with a diffident sense of intrusion, conscious that his standing as a member might not be recognised by the keepers of the doors; in a moment, however, he realised that a rajah's escort of elephants might almost have marched through the entrance hall and vestibule without challenge. The general atmosphere of the scene suggested a blend of the railway station at Cologne, the Hotel Bristol in any European capital, and the second act in most musical comedies. A score of brilliant and brilliantined pages decorated the foreground, while Hebraic-looking gentlemen, wearing tartan waistcoats of the clans of their adoption, flitted restlessly between the tape machines and telephone boxes. The army of occupation had obviously established a firm footing in the hospitable premises; a kaleidoscopic pattern of uniforms, sky-blue, indigo, and bottle-green, relieved the civilian attire of the groups that clustered in lounge and card rooms and corridors. Yeovil rapidly came to the conclusion that the joys of membership were not for him. He had turned to go, after a very cursory inspection of the premises and their human occupants, when he was hailed by a young man, dressed with strenuous neatness, whom he remembered having met in past days at the houses of one or two common friends.

Hubert Herlton's parents had brought him into the world, and some twenty-one years later had put him into a motor business. Having taken these pardonable liberties they had completely exhausted their ideas of what to do with him, and Hubert seemed unlikely to develop any ideas of his own on the subject. The motor business elected to conduct itself without his connivance; journalism, the stage, tomato culture (without capital), and other professions that could be entered on at short notice were submitted to his consideration by nimble-minded relations and friends. He listened to their suggestions with polite indifference, being rude only to a cousin who demonstrated how he might achieve a settled income of from two hundred to a thousand pounds a year by the propagation of mushrooms in a London basement. While his walk in life was still an undetermined promenade his parents died, leaving him with a carefully-invested income of thirty-seven pounds a year. At that point of his career Yeovil's knowledge of him stopped short; the journey to Siberia had taken him beyond the range of Herlton's domestic vicissitudes.

The young man greeted him in a decidedly friendly manner.

"I didn't know you were a member here," he exclaimed.

"It's the first time I've ever been in the club," said Yeovil, "and I fancy it will be the last. There is rather too much of the fighting machine in evidence here. One doesn't want a perpetual reminder of what has happened staring one in the face."

"We tried at first to keep the alien element out," said Herlton apologetically, "but we couldn't have carried on the club if we'd stuck to that line. You see we'd lost more than two-thirds of our old members so we couldn't afford to be exclusive. As a matter of fact the whole thing was decided over our heads; a new syndicate took over the concern, and a new committee was installed, with a good many foreigners on it. I know it's horrid having these uniforms flaunting all over the place, but what is one to do?"

Yeovil said nothing, with the air of a man who could have said a great deal.

"I suppose you wonder, why remain a member under those conditions?" continued Herlton. "Well, as far as I am concerned, a place like this is a necessity for me. In fact, it's my profession, my source of income."

"Are you as good at bridge as all that?" asked Yeovil; "I'm a fairly successful player myself, but I should be sorry to have to live on my winnings, year in, year out."

"I don't play cards," said Herlton, "at least not for serious stakes. My winnings or losings wouldn't come to a tenner in an average year. No, I live by commissions, by introducing likely buyers to would-be sellers."

"Sellers of what?" asked Yeovil.

"Anything, everything; horses, yachts, old masters, plate, shootings, poultry-farms, week-end cottages, motor cars, almost anything you can think of. Look," and he produced from his breast pocket a bulky note-book illusorily inscribed "engagements."

"Here," he explained, tapping the book, "I've got a double entry of every likely client that I know, with a note of the things he may have to sell and the things he may want to buy. When it is something that he has for sale there are cross-references to likely purchasers of that particular line of article. I don't limit myself to things that I actually know people to be in want of, I go further than that and have theories, carefully indexed theories, as to the things that people might want to buy. At the right moment, if I can get the opportunity, I mention the article that is in my mind's eye to the possible purchaser who has also been in my mind's eye, and I frequently bring off a sale. I started a chance acquaintance on a career of print-buying the other day merely by telling him of a couple of good prints that I knew of, that were to be had at a quite reasonable price; he is a man with more money than he knows what to do with, and he has laid out quite a lot on old prints since his first purchase. Most of his collection he has got through me, and of course I net a commission on each transaction. So you see, old man, how useful, not to say necessary, a club with a large membership is to me. The more mixed and socially chaotic it is, the more serviceable it is."

"Of course," said Yeovil, "and I suppose, as a matter of fact, a good many of your clients belong to the conquering race."

"Well, you see, they are the people who have got the money," said Herlton; "I don't mean to say that the invading Germans are usually people of wealth, but while they live over here they escape the crushing taxation that falls on the British-born subject. They serve their country as soldiers, and we have to serve it in garrison money, ship money and so forth, besides the ordinary taxes of the State. The German shoulders the rifle, the Englishman has to shoulder everything else. That is what will help more than anything towards the gradual Germanising of our big towns; the comparatively lightly-taxed German workman over here will have a much bigger spending power and purchasing power than his heavily taxed English neighbour. The public-houses, bars, eating-houses, places of amusement and so forth, will come to cater more and more for money-yielding German patronage. The stream of British emigration will swell rather than diminish, and the stream of Teuton immigration will be equally persistent and progressive. Yes, the military-service ordinance was a cunning stroke on the part of that old fox, von Kwarl. As a civilian statesman he is far and away cleverer than Bismarck was; he smothers with a feather-bed where Bismarck would have tried to smash with a sledge-hammer."

"Have you got me down on your list of noteworthy people?" asked Yeovil, turning the drift of the conversation back to the personal topic.

"Certainly I have," said Herlton, turning the pages of his pocket directory to the letter Y. "As soon as I knew you were back in England I made several entries concerning you. In the first place it was possible that you might have a volume on Siberian travel and natural history notes to publish, and I've cross-referenced you to a publisher I know who rather wants books of that sort on his list."

"I may tell you at once that I've no intentions in that direction," said Yeovil, in some amusement.

"Just as well," said Herlton cheerfully, scribbling a hieroglyphic in his book; "that branch of business is rather outside my line—too little in it, and the gratitude of author and publisher for being introduced to one another is usually short-lived. A more serious entry was the item that if you were wintering in England you would be looking out for a hunter or two. You used to hunt with the East Wessex, I remember; I've got just the very animal that will suit that country, ready waiting for you. A beautiful clean jumper. I've put it over a fence or two myself, and you and I ride much the same weight. A stiffish price is being asked for it, but I've got the letters D.O. after your name."

"In Heaven's name," said Yeovil, now openly grinning, "before I die of curiosity tell me what D.O. stands for."

"It means some one who doesn't object to pay a good price for anything that really suits him. There are some people of course who won't consider a thing unless they can get it for about a third of what they imagine to be its market value. I've got another suggestion down against you in my book; you may not be staying in the country at all, you may be clearing out in disgust at existing conditions. In that case you would be selling a lot of things that you wouldn't want to cart away with you. That involves another set of entries and a whole lot of cross references."

"I'm afraid I've given you a lot of trouble," said Yeovil drily.

"Not at all," said Herlton, "but it would simplify matters if we take it for granted that you are going to stay here, for this winter anyhow, and are looking out for hunters. Can you lunch with me here on Wednesday, and come and look at the animal afterwards? It's only thirty-five minutes by train. It will take us longer if we motor. There is a two-fifty-three from Charing Cross that we could catch comfortably."

"If you are going to persuade me to hunt in the East Wessex country this season," said Yeovil, "you must find me a convenient hunting box somewhere down there."

"I have found it," said Herlton, whipping out a stylograph, and hastily scribbling an "order to view" on a card; "central as possible for all the meets, grand stabling accommodation, excellent water-supply, big bathroom, game larder, cellarage, a bakehouse if you want to bake your own bread—"

"Any land with it?"

"Not enough to be a nuisance. An acre or two of paddock and about the same of garden. You are fond of wild things; a wood comes down to the edge of the garden, a wood that harbours owls and buzzards and kestrels."

"Have you got all those details in your book?" asked Yeovil; "'wood adjoining property, O.B.K.'"

"I keep those details in my head," said Herlton, "but they are quite reliable."

"I shall insist on something substantial off the rent if there are no buzzards," said Yeovil; "now that you have mentioned them they seem an indispensable accessory to any decent hunting-box. Look," he exclaimed, catching sight of a plump middle-aged individual, crossing the vestibule with an air of restrained importance, "there goes the delectable Pitherby. Does he come on your books at all?"

"I should say!" exclaimed Herlton fervently. "The delectable P. nourishes expectations of a barony or viscounty at an early date. Most of his life has been spent in streets and squares, with occasional migrations to the esplanades of fashionable watering-places or the gravelled walks of country house gardens. Now that noblesse is about to impose its obligations on him, quite a new catalogue of wants has sprung into his mind. There are things that a plain esquire may leave undone without causing scandalised remark, but a fiercer light beats on a baron. Trigger-pulling is one of the obligations. Up to the present Pitherby has never hit a partridge in anger, but this year he has commissioned me to rent him a deer forest. Some pedigree Herefords for his 'home farm' was another commission, and a dozen and a half swans for a swannery. The swannery, I may say, was my idea; I said once in his hearing that it gave a baronial air to an estate; you see I knew a man who had got a lot of surplus swan stock for sale. Now Pitherby wants a heronry as well. I've put him in communication with a client of mine who suffers from superfluous herons, but of course I can't guarantee that the birds' nesting arrangements will fall in with his territorial requirement. I'm getting him some carp, too, of quite respectable age, for a carp pond; I thought it would look so well for his lady-wife to be discovered by interviewers feeding the carp with her own fair hands, and I put the same idea into Pitherby's mind."

"I had no idea that so many things were necessary to endorse a patent of nobility," said Yeovil. "If there should be any miscarriage in the bestowal of the honour at least Pitherby will have absolved himself from any charge of contributory negligence."

"Shall we say Wednesday, here, one o'clock, lunch first, and go down and look at the horse afterwards?" said Herlton, returning to the matter in hand.

Yeovil hesitated, then he nodded his head.

"There is no harm in going to look at the animal," he said.

XVI

Sunrise

Mrs. Kerrick sat at a little teak-wood table in the verandah of a low-pitched teak-built house that stood on the steep slope of a brown hillside. Her youngest child, with the grave natural dignity of nine-year old girlhood, maintained a correct but observant silence, looking carefully yet unobtrusively after the wants of the one guest, and checking from time to time the incursions of ubiquitous ants that were obstinately disposed to treat the table-cloth as a foraging ground. The wayfaring visitor, who was experiencing a British blend of Eastern hospitality, was a French naturalist, travelling thus far afield in quest of feathered specimens to enrich the aviaries of a bird-collecting Balkan King. On the previous evening, while shrugging his shoulders and unloosing his vocabulary over the meagre accommodation afforded by the native rest-house, he had been enchanted by receiving an invitation to transfer his quarters to the house on the hillside, where he found not only a pleasant-voiced hostess and some drinkable wine, but three brown-skinned English youngsters who were able to give him a mass of intelligent first-hand information about the bird life of the region. And now, at the early morning breakfast, ere yet the sun was showing over the rim of the brown-baked hills, he was learning something of the life of the little community he had chanced on. "I was in these parts many years ago," explained the hostess, "when my husband was alive and had an appointment out here. It is a healthy hill district and I had pleasant memories of the place, so when it became necessary, well, desirable let us say, to leave our English home and find a new one, it occurred to me to bring my boys and my little girl here—my eldest girl is at school in Paris. Labour is cheap here and I try my hand at farming in a small way. Of course it is very different work to just superintending the dairy and poultry-yard arrangements of an English country estate. There are so many things, insect ravages, bird depredations, and so on, that one only knows on a small scale in England, that happen here in wholesale fashion, not to mention droughts and torrential rains and other tropical visitations. And then the domestic animals are so disconcertingly different from the ones one has been used to; humped cattle never seem to behave in the way that straight-backed cattle would, and goats and geese and chickens are not a bit the same here that they are in Europe— and of course the farm servants are utterly unlike the same class in England. One has to unlearn a good deal of what one thought one knew about stock-keeping and agriculture, and take note of the native ways of doing things; they are primitive and unenterprising of course, but they have an accumulated store of experience behind them, and one has to tread warily in initiating improvements."

The Frenchman looked round at the brown sun-scorched hills, with the dusty empty road showing here and there in the middle distance and other brown sun-scorched hills rounding off the scene; he looked at the lizards on the verandah walls, at the jars for keeping the water cool, at the numberless little insect-bored holes in the furniture, at the heat-drawn lines on his hostess's comely face. Notwithstanding his present wanderings he had a Frenchman's strong homing instinct, and he marvelled to hear this lady, who should have been a lively and popular figure in the social circle of some English county town, talking serenely of the ways of humped cattle and native servants.

"And your children, how do they like the change?" he asked.

"It is healthy up here among the hills," said the mother, also looking round at the landscape and thinking doubtless of a very different scene; "they have an outdoor life and plenty of liberty. They have their ponies to ride, and there is a lake up above us that is a fine place for them to bathe and boat in; the three boys are there now, having their morning swim. The eldest is sixteen and he is allowed to have a gun, and there is some good wild fowl shooting to be had in the reed beds at the further end of the lake. I think that part of the joy of his shooting expeditions lies in the fact that many of the duck and plover that he comes across belong to the same species that frequent our English moors and rivers."

It was the first hint that she had given of a wistful sense of exile, the yearning for other skies, the message that a dead bird's plumage could bring across rolling seas and scorching plains.

"And the education of your boys, how do you manage for that?" asked the visitor.

"There is a young tutor living out in these wilds," said Mrs. Kerrick; "he was assistant master at a private school in Scotland, but it had to be given up when—when things changed; so many of the boys left the country. He came out to an uncle who has a small estate eight miles from here, and three days in the week he rides over to teach my boys, and three days he goes to another family living in the opposite direction. Today he is due to come here. It is a great boon to have such an opportunity for getting the boys educated, and of course it helps him to earn a living."

"And the society of the place?" asked the Frenchman.

His hostess laughed.

"I must admit it has to be looked for with a strong pair of field-glasses," she said; "it is almost as difficult to get a good bridge four together as it would have been to get up a tennis tournament or a subscription dance in our particular corner of England. One has to ignore distances and forget fatigue if one wants to be gregarious even on a limited scale. There are one or two officials who are our chief social mainstays, but the difficulty is to muster the few available souls under the same roof at the same moment. A road will be impassable in one quarter, a pony will be lame in another, a stress of work will prevent some one else from coming, and another may be down with a touch of fever. When my little girl gave a birthday party here her only little girl guest had come twelve miles to attend it. The Forest officer happened to drop in on us that evening, so we felt quite festive."

The Frenchman's eyes grew round in wonder. He had once thought that the capital city of a Balkan kingdom was the uttermost limit of social desolation, viewed from a Parisian standpoint, and there at any rate one could get cafe chantant, tennis, picnic parties, an occasional theatre performance by a foreign troupe, now and then a travelling circus, not to speak of Court and diplomatic functions of a more or less sociable character. Here, it seemed, one went a day's journey to reach an evening's entertainment, and the chance arrival of a tired official took on the nature of a festivity. He looked round again at the rolling stretches of brown hills; before he had regarded them merely as the background to this little shut-away world, now he saw that they were foreground as well. They were everything, there was nothing else. And again his glance travelled to the face of his hostess, with its bright, pleasant eyes and smiling mouth.

"And you live here with your children," he said, "here in this wilderness? You leave England, you leave everything, for this?"

His hostess rose and took him over to the far side of the verandah. The beginnings of a garden were spread out before them, with young fruit trees and flowering shrubs, and bushes of pale pink roses. Exuberant tropical growths were interspersed with carefully tended vestiges of plants that had evidently been brought from a more temperate climate, and had not borne the transition well. Bushes and trees and shrubs spread away for some distance, to where the ground rose in a small hillock and then fell away abruptly into bare hillside.

"In all this garden that you see," said the Englishwoman, "there is one tree that is sacred."

"A tree?" said the Frenchman.

"A tree that we could not grow in England."

The Frenchman followed the direction of her eyes and saw a tall, bare pole at the summit of the hillock. At the same moment the sun came over the hilltops in a deep, orange glow, and a new light stole like magic over the brown landscape. And, as if they had timed their arrival to that exact moment of sunburst, three brown-faced boys appeared under the straight, bare pole. A cord shivered and flapped, and something ran swiftly up into the air, and swung out in the breeze that blew across the hills—a blue flag with red and white crosses. The three boys bared their heads and the small girl on the verandah steps stood rigidly to attention. Far away down the hill, a young man, cantering into view round a corner of the dusty road, removed his hat in loyal salutation.

"That is why we live out here," said the Englishwoman quietly.

XVII

The Event of the Season

In the first swelter room of the new Osmanli Baths in Cork Street four or five recumbent individuals, in a state of moist nudity and self-respecting inertia, were smoking cigarettes or making occasional pretence of reading damp newspapers. A glass wall with a glass door shut them off from the yet more torrid regions of the further swelter chambers; another glass partition disclosed the dimly-lit vault where other patrons of the establishment had arrived at the stage of being pounded and kneaded and sluiced by Oriental-looking attendants. The splashing and trickling of taps, the flip-flap of wet slippers on a wet floor, and the low murmur of conversation, filtered through glass doors, made an appropriately drowsy accompaniment to the scene.

A new-comer fluttered into the room, beamed at one of the occupants, and settled himself with an air of elaborate languor in a long canvas chair. Cornelian Valpy was a fair young man, with perpetual surprise impinged on his countenance, and a chin that seemed to have retired from competition with the rest of his features. The beam of recognition that he had given to his friend or acquaintance subsided into a subdued but lingering simper.

"What is the matter?" drawled his neighbour lazily, dropping the end of a cigarette into a small bowl of water, and helping himself from a silver case on the table at his side.

"Matter?" said Cornelian, opening wide a pair of eyes in which unhealthy intelligence seemed to struggle in undetermined battle with utter vacuity; "why should you suppose that anything is the matter?"

"When you wear a look of idiotic complacency in a Turkish bath," said the other, "it is the more noticeable from the fact that you are wearing nothing else."

"Were you at the Shalem House dance last night?" asked Cornelian, by way of explaining his air of complacent retrospection.

"No," said the other, "but I feel as if I had been; I've been reading columns about it in the Dawn."

"The last event of the season," said Cornelian, "and quite one of the most amusing and lively functions that there have been."

"So the Dawn said; but then, as Shalem practically owns and controls that paper, its favourable opinion might be taken for granted."

"The whole idea of the Revel was quite original," said Cornelian, who was not going to have his personal narrative of the event forestalled by anything that a newspaper reporter might have given to the public; "a certain number of guests went as famous personages in the world's history, and each one was accompanied by another guest typifying the prevailing characteristic of that personage. One man went as Julius Caesar, for instance, and had a girl typifying ambition as his shadow, another went as Louis the Eleventh, and his companion personified superstition. Your shadow had to be someone of the opposite sex, you see, and every alternate dance throughout the evening you danced with your shadow-partner. Quite a clever idea; young Graf von Schnatelstein is supposed to have invented it."

"New York will be deeply beholden to him," said the other; "shadow-dances, with all manner of eccentric variations, will be the rage there for the next eighteen months."

"Some of the costumes were really sumptuous," continued Cornelian; "the Duchess of Dreyshire was magnificent as Aholibah, you never saw so many jewels on one person, only of course she didn't look dark enough for the character; she had Billy Carnset for her shadow, representing Unspeakable Depravity."

"How on earth did he manage that?"

"Oh, a blend of Beardsley and Bakst as far as get-up and costume, and of course his own personality counted for a good deal. Quite one of the successes of the evening was Leutnant von Gabelroth, as George Washington, with Joan Mardle as his shadow, typifying Inconvenient Candour. He put her down officially as Truthfulness, but every one had heard the other version."

"Good for the Gabelroth, though he does belong to the invading Horde; it's not often that any one scores off Joan."

"Another blaze of magnificence was the loud-voiced Bessimer woman, as the Goddess Juno, with peacock tails and opals all over her; she had Ronnie Storre to represent Green-eyed Jealousy. Talking of Ronnie Storre and of jealousy, you will naturally wonder whom Mrs. Yeovil went with. I forget what her costume was, but she'd got that dark-headed youth with her that she's been trotting round everywhere the last few days."

Cornelian's neighbour kicked him furtively on the shin, and frowned in the direction of a dark-haired youth reclining in an adjacent chair.

The youth in question rose from his seat and stalked into the further swelter room.

"So clever of him to go into the furnace room," said the unabashed Cornelian; "now if he turns scarlet all over we shall never know how much is embarrassment and how much is due to the process of being boiled. La Yeovil hasn't done badly by the exchange; he's better looking than Ronnie."

"I see that Pitherby went as Frederick the Great," said Cornelian's neighbour, fingering a sheet of the Dawn.

"Isn't that exactly what one would have expected Pitherby to do?" said Cornelian. "He's so desperately anxious to announce to all whom it may concern that he has written a life of that hero. He had an uninspiring-looking woman with him, supposed to represent Military Genius."

"The Spirit of Advertisement would have been more appropriate," said the other.

"The opening scene of the Revel was rather effective," continued Cornelian; "all the Shadow people reclined in the dimly-lit centre of the ballroom in an indistinguishable mass, and the human characters marched round the illuminated sides of the room to solemn processional music. Every now and then a shadow would detach itself from the mass, hail its partner by name, and glide out to join him or her in the procession. Then, when the last shadows had found their mates and every one was partnered, the lights were turned up in a blaze, the orchestra crashed out a whirl of nondescript dance music, and people just let themselves go. It was Pandemonium. Afterwards every one strutted about for half an hour or so, showing themselves off, and then the legitimate programme of dances began. There were some rather amusing incidents throughout the evening. One set of lancers was danced entirely by the Seven Deadly Sins and their human exemplars; of course seven couples were not sufficient to make up the set, so they had to bring in an eighth sin, I forget what it was."

"The sin of Patriotism would have been rather appropriate, considering who were giving the dance," said the other.

"Hush!" exclaimed Cornelian nervously. "You don't know who may overhear you in a place like this. You'll get yourself into trouble."

"Wasn't there some rather daring new dance of the 'bunny-hug' variety?" asked the indiscreet one.

"The 'Cubby-Cuddle,'" said Cornelian; "three or four adventurous couples danced it towards the end of the evening."

"The Dawn says that without being strikingly new it was strikingly modern."

"The best description I can give of it," said Cornelian, "is summed up in the comment of the Grafin von Tolb when she saw it being danced: 'if they really love each other I suppose it doesn't matter.' By the way," he added with apparent indifference, "is there any detailed account of my costume in the Dawn?"

His companion laughed cynically.

"As if you hadn't read everything that the Dawn and the other morning papers have to say about the ball hours ago."

"The naked truth should be avoided in a Turkish bath," said Cornelian; "kindly assume that I've only had time to glance at the weather forecast and the news from China."

"Oh, very well," said the other; "your costume isn't described; you simply come amid a host of others as 'Mr. Cornelian Valpy, resplendent as the Emperor Nero; with him Miss Kate Lerra, typifying Insensate Vanity.' Many hard things have been said of Nero, but his unkindest critics have never accused him of resembling you in feature. Until some very clear evidence is produced I shall refuse to believe it."

Cornelian was proof against these shafts; leaning back gracefully in his chair he launched forth into that detailed description of his last night's attire which the Dawn had so unaccountably failed to supply.

"I wore a tunic of white Nepaulese silk, with a collar of pearls, real pearls. Round my waist I had a girdle of twisted serpents in beaten gold, studded all over with amethysts. My sandals were of gold, laced with scarlet thread, and I had seven bracelets of gold on each arm. Round my head I had a wreath of golden laurel leaves set with scarlet berries, and hanging over my left shoulder was a silk robe of mulberry purple, broidered with the signs of the zodiac in gold and scarlet; I had it made specially for the occasion. At my side I had an ivory-sheathed dagger, with a green jade handle, hung in a green Cordova leather—"

At this point of the recital his companion rose softly, flung his cigarette end into the little water-bowl, and passed into the further swelter room. Cornelian Valpy was left, still clothed in a look of ineffable complacency, still engaged, in all probability, in reclothing himself in the finery of the previous evening.

XVIII

The Dead Who Do Not Understand

The pale light of a November afternoon faded rapidly into the dusk of a November evening. Far over the countryside housewives put up their cottage shutters, lit their lamps, and made the customary remark that the days were drawing in. In barn yards and poultry-runs the greediest pullets made a final tour of inspection, picking up the stray remaining morsels of the evening meal, and then, with much scrambling and squawking, sought the places on the roosting-pole that they thought should belong to them. Labourers working in yard and field began to turn their thoughts homeward or tavernward as the case might be. And through the cold squelching slush of a water-logged meadow a weary, bedraggled, but unbeaten fox stiffly picked his way, climbed a high bramble-grown bank, and flung himself into the sheltering labyrinth of a stretching tangle of woods. The pack of fierce-mouthed things that had rattled him from copse and gorse-cover, along fallow and plough, hedgerow and wooded lane, for nigh on an hour, and had pressed hard on his life for the last few minutes, receded suddenly into the background of his experiences. The cold, wet meadow, the thick mask of woods, and the oncoming dusk had stayed the chase—and the fox had outstayed it. In a short time he would fall mechanically to licking off some of the mud that caked on his weary pads; in a shorter time horsemen and hounds would have drawn off kennelward and homeward.

Yeovil rode through the deepening twilight, relying chiefly on his horse to find its way in the network of hedge-bordered lanes that presumably led to a high road or to some human habitation. He was desperately tired after his day's hunting, a legacy of weakness that the fever had bequeathed to him, but even though he could scarcely sit upright in his saddle his mind dwelt complacently on the day's sport and looked forward to the snug cheery comfort that awaited him at his hunting box. There was a charm, too, even for a tired man, in the eerie stillness of the lone twilight land through which he was passing, a grey shadow-hung land which seemed to have been emptied of all things that belonged to the daytime, and filled with a lurking, moving life of which one knew nothing beyond the sense that it was there. There, and very near. If there had been wood-gods and wicked-eyed fauns in the sunlit groves and hill sides of old Hellas, surely there were watchful, living things of kindred mould in this dusk-hidden wilderness of field and hedge and coppice.

It was Yeovil's third or fourth day with the hounds, without taking into account a couple of mornings' cub-hunting. Already he felt that he had been doing nothing different from this all his life. His foreign travels, his illness, his recent weeks in London, they were part of a tapestried background that had very slight and distant connection with his present existence. Of the future he tried to think with greater energy and determination. For this winter, at any rate, he would hunt and do a little shooting, entertain a few of his neighbours and make friends with any congenial fellow-sportsmen who might be within reach. Next year things would be different; he would have had time to look round him, to regain something of his aforetime vigour of mind and body. Next year, when the hunting season was over, he would set about finding out whether there was any nobler game for him to take a hand in. He would enter into correspondence with old friends who had gone out into the tropics and the backwoods—he would do something.

So he told himself, but he knew thoroughly well that he had found his level. He had ceased to struggle against the fascination of his present surroundings. The slow, quiet comfort and interest of country life appealed with enervating force to the man whom death had half conquered. The pleasures of the chase, well-provided for in every detail, and dovetailed in with the assured luxury of a well-ordered, well-staffed establishment, were exactly what he wanted and exactly what his life down here afforded him. He was experiencing, too, that passionate recurring devotion to an old loved scene that comes at times to men who have travelled far and willingly up and down the world. He was very much at home. The alien standard floating over Buckingham Palace, the Crown of Charlemagne on public buildings and official documents, the grey ships of war riding in Plymouth Bay and Southampton Water with a flag at their stern that older generations of Britons had never looked on, these things seemed far away and inconsequent amid the hedgerows and woods and fallows of the East Wessex country. Horse and hound-craft, harvest, game broods, the planting and felling of timber, the rearing and selling of stock, the letting of grasslands, the care of fisheries, the up-keep of markets and fairs, they were the things that immediately mattered. And Yeovil saw himself, in moments of disgust and self-accusation, settling down into this life of rustic littleness, concerned over the late nesting of a partridge or the defective draining of a loose-box, hugely busy over affairs that a gardener's boy might grapple with, ignoring the struggle-cry that went up, low and bitter and wistful, from a dethroned dispossessed race, in whose glories he had gloried, in whose struggle he lent no hand. In what way, he asked himself in such moments, would his life be better than the life of that parody of manhood who upholstered his rooms with art hangings and rosewood furniture and babbled over the effect?

The lanes seemed interminable and without aim or object except to bisect one another; gates and gaps disclosed nothing in the way of a landmark, and the night began to draw down in increasing shades of darkness. Presently, however, the tired horse quickened its pace, swung round a sharp corner into a broader roadway, and stopped with an air of thankful expectancy at the low doorway of a wayside inn. A cheerful glow of light streamed from the windows and door, and a brighter glare came from the other side of the road, where a large motorcar was being got ready for an immediate start. Yeovil tumbled stiffly out of his saddle, and in answer to the loud rattle of his hunting crop on the open door the innkeeper and two or three hangers-on hurried out to attend to the wants of man and beast. Flour and water for the horse and something hot for himself were Yeovil's first concern, and then he began to clamour for geographical information. He was rather dismayed to find that the cumulative opinions of those whom he consulted, and of several others who joined unbidden in the discussion, placed his destination at nothing nearer than nine miles. Nine miles of dark and hilly country road for a tired man on a tired horse assumed enormous, far-stretching proportions, and although he dimly remembered that he had asked a guest to dinner for that evening he began to wonder whether the wayside inn possessed anything endurable in the way of a bedroom. The landlord interrupted his desperate speculations with a really brilliant effort of suggestion. There was a gentleman in the bar, he said, who was going in a motorcar in the direction for which Yeovil was bound, and who would no doubt be willing to drop him at his destination; the gentleman had also been out with the hounds. Yeovil's horse could be stabled at the inn and fetched home by a groom the next morning. A hurried embassy to the bar parlour resulted in the news that the motorist would be delighted to be of assistance to a fellow-sportsman.

Yeovil gratefully accepted the chance that had so obligingly come his way, and hastened to superintend the housing of his horse in its night's quarters. When he had duly seen to the tired animal's comfort and foddering he returned to the roadway, where a young man in hunting garb and a livened chauffeur were standing by the side of the waiting car.

"I am so very pleased to be of some use to you, Mr. Yeovil," said the car-owner, with a polite bow, and Yeovil recognised the young Leutnant von Gabelroth, who had been present at the musical afternoon at Berkshire Street. He had doubtless seen him at the meet that morning, but in his hunting kit he had escaped his observation.

"I, too, have been out with the hounds," the young man continued; "I have left my horse at the Crow and Sceptre at Dolford. You are living at Black Dene, are you not? I can take you right past your door, it is all on my way."

Yeovil hung back for a moment, overwhelmed with vexation and embarrassment, but it was too late to cancel the arrangement he had unwittingly entered into, and he was constrained to put himself under obligation to the young officer with the best grace he could muster. After all, he reflected, he had met him under his own roof as his wife's guest. He paid his reckoning to mine host, tipped the stable lad who had helped him with his horse, and took his place beside von Gabelroth in the car.

As they glided along the dark roadway and the young German reeled off a string of comments on the incidents of the day's sport, Yeovil lay back amid his comfortable wraps and weighed the measure of his humiliation. It was Cicely's gospel that one should know what one wanted in life and take good care that one got what one wanted. Could he apply that test of achievement to his own life? Was this what he really wanted to be doing, pursuing his uneventful way as a country squire, sharing even his sports and pastimes with men of the nation that had conquered and enslaved his Fatherland?

The car slackened its pace somewhat as they went through a small hamlet, past a schoolhouse, past a rural police-station with the new monogram over its notice-board, past a church with a little tree-grown graveyard. There, in a corner, among wild-rose bushes and tall yews, lay some of Yeovil's own kinsfolk, who had lived in these parts and hunted and found life pleasant in the days that were not so very long ago. Whenever he went past that quiet little gathering-place of the dead Yeovil was wont to raise his hat in mute affectionate salutation to those who were now only memories in his family; tonight he somehow omitted the salute and turned his head the other way. It was as though the dead of his race saw and wondered.

Three or four months ago the thing he was doing would have seemed an impossibility, now it was actually happening; he was listening to the gay, courteous, tactful chatter of his young companion, laughing now and then at some joking remark, answering some question of interest, learning something of hunting ways and traditions in von Gabelroth's own country. And when the car turned in at the gate of the hunting lodge and drew up at the steps the laws of hospitality demanded that Yeovil should ask his benefactor of the road to come in for a few minutes and drink something a little better than the wayside inn had been able to supply. The young officer spent the best part of a half hour in Yeovil's snuggery, examining and discussing the trophies of rifle and collecting gun that covered the walls. He had a good knowledge of woodcraft, and the beasts and birds of Siberian forests and North African deserts were to him new pages in a familiar book. Yeovil found himself discoursing eagerly with his chance guest on the European distribution and local variation of such and such a species, recounting peculiarities in its habits and incidents of its pursuit and capture. If the cold observant eyes of Lady Shalem could have rested on the scene she would have hailed it as another root-fibre thrown out by the fait accompli.

Yeovil closed the hall door on his departing visitor, and closed his mind on the crowd of angry and accusing thoughts that were waiting to intrude themselves. His valet had already got his bath in readiness and in a few minutes the tired huntsman was forgetting weariness and the consciousness of outside things in the languorous abandonment that steam and hot water induce. Brain and limbs seemed to lay themselves down in a contented waking sleep, the world that was beyond the bathroom walls dropped away into a far unreal distance; only somewhere through the steam clouds pierced a hazy consciousness that a dinner, well chosen, was being well cooked, and would presently be well served—and right well appreciated. That was the lure to drag the bather away from the Nirvana land of warmth and steam. The stimulating after-effect of the bath took its due effect, and Yeovil felt that he was now much less tired and enormously hungry. A cheery fire burned in his dressing-room and a lively black kitten helped him to dress, and incidentally helped him to require a new tassel to the cord of his dressing-gown. As he finished his toilet and the kitten finished its sixth and most notable attack on the tassel a ring was heard at the front door, and a moment later a loud, hearty, and unmistakably hungry voice resounded in the hall. It belonged to the local doctor, who had also taken part in the day's run and had been bidden to enliven the evening meal with the entertainment of his inexhaustible store of sporting and social reminiscences. He knew the countryside and the countryfolk inside out, and he was a living unwritten chronicle of the East Wessex hunt. His conversation seemed exactly the right accompaniment to the meal; his stories brought glimpses of wet hedgerows, stiff ploughlands, leafy spinneys and muddy brooks in among the rich old Worcester and Georgian silver of the dinner service, the glow and crackle of the wood fire, the pleasant succession of well-cooked dishes and mellow wines. The world narrowed itself down again to a warm, drowsy-scented dining-room, with a productive hinterland of kitchen and cellar beyond it, and beyond that an important outer world of loose box and harness-room and stable-yard; further again a dark hushed region where pheasants roosted and owls flitted and foxes prowled.

Yeovil sat and listened to story after story of the men and women and horses of the neighbourhood; even the foxes seemed to have a personality, some of them, and a personal history. It was a little like Hans Andersen, he decided, and a little like the Reminiscences of an Irish R.M., and perhaps just a little like some of the more probable adventures of Baron Munchausen. The newer stories were evidently true to the smallest detail, the earlier ones had altered somewhat in repetition, as plants and animals vary under domestication.

And all the time there was one topic that was never touched on. Of half the families mentioned it was necessary to add the qualifying information that they "used to live" at such and such a place; the countryside knew them no longer. Their properties were for sale or had already passed into the hands of strangers. But neither man cared to allude to the grinning shadow that sat at the feast and sent an icy chill now and again through the cheeriest jest and most jovial story. The brisk run with the hounds that day had stirred and warmed their pulses; it was an evening for comfortable forgetting. Later that night, in the stillness of his bedroom, with the dwindling noises of a retiring household dropping off one by one into ordered silence, a door shutting here, a fire being raked out there, the thoughts that had been held away came crowding in. The body was tired, but the brain was not, and Yeovil lay awake with his thoughts for company. The world grew suddenly wide again, filled with the significance of things that mattered, held by the actions of men that mattered. Hunting-box and stable and gun-room dwindled to a mere pin-point in the universe, there were other larger, more absorbing things on which the mind dwelt. There was the grey cold sea outside Dover and Portsmouth and Cork, where the great grey ships of war rocked and swung with the tides, where the sailors sang, in doggerel English, that bitter-sounding adaptation, "Germania rules t'e waves," where the flag of a World-Power floated for the world to see. And in oven-like cities of India there were men who looked out at the white sun-glare, the heat-baked dust, the welter of crowded streets, who listened to the unceasing chorus of harsh-throated crows, the strident creaking of cart-wheels, the buzz and drone of insect swarms and the rattle call of the tree lizards; men whose thoughts went hungrily to the cool grey skies and wet turf and moist ploughlands of an English hunting country, men whose memories listened yearningly to the music of a deep-throated hound and the call of a game-bird in the stubble. Yeovil had secured for himself the enjoyment of the things for which these men hungered; he had known what he wanted in life, slowly and with hesitation, yet nevertheless surely, he had arrived at the achievement of his unconfessed desires. Here, installed under his own roof-tree, with as good horseflesh in his stable as man could desire, with sport lying almost at his door, with his wife ready to come down and help him to entertain his neighbours, Murrey Yeovil had found the life that he wanted—and was accursed in his own eyes. He argued with himself, and palliated and explained, but he knew why he had turned his eyes away that evening from the little graveyard under the trees; one cannot explain things to the dead.

XIX

The Little Foxes

"Take us the foxes, the little foxes, that spoil the vines"

On a warm and sunny May afternoon, some ten months since Yeovil's return from his Siberian wanderings and sickness, Cicely sat at a small table in the open-air restaurant in Hyde Park, finishing her after-luncheon coffee and listening to the meritorious performance of the orchestra. Opposite her sat Larry Meadowfield, absorbed for the moment in the slow enjoyment of a cigarette, which also was not without its short-lived merits. Larry was a well-dressed youngster, who was, in Cicely's opinion, distinctly good to look on—an opinion which the boy himself obviously shared. He had the healthy, well-cared-for appearance of a country-dweller who has been turned into a town dandy without suffering in the process. His blue-black hair, growing very low down on a broad forehead, was brushed back in a smoothness that gave his head the appearance of a rain-polished sloe; his eyebrows were two dark smudges and his large violet-grey eyes expressed the restful good temper of an animal whose immediate requirements have been satisfied. The lunch had been an excellent one, and it was jolly to feed out of doors in the warm spring air—the only drawback to the arrangement being the absence of mirrors. However, if he could not look at himself a great many people could look at him.

Cicely listened to the orchestra as it jerked and strutted through a fantastic dance measure, and as she listened she looked appreciatively at the boy on the other side of the table, whose soul for the moment seemed to be in his cigarette. Her scheme of life, knowing just what you wanted and taking good care that you got it, was justifying itself by results. Ronnie, grown tiresome with success, had not been difficult to replace, and no one in her world had had the satisfaction of being able to condole with her on the undesirable experience of a long interregnum. To feminine acquaintances with fewer advantages of purse and brains and looks she might figure as "that Yeovil woman," but never had she given them justification to allude to her as "poor Cicely Yeovil." And Murrey, dear old soul, had cooled down, as she had hoped and wished, from his white heat of disgust at the things that she had prepared herself to accept philosophically. A new chapter of their married life and man-and-woman friendship had opened; many a rare gallop they had had together that winter, many a cheery dinner gathering and long bridge evening in the cosy hunting-lodge. Though he still hated the new London and held himself aloof from most of her Town set, yet he had not shown himself rigidly intolerant of the sprinkling of Teuton sportsmen who hunted and shot down in his part of the country.

The orchestra finished its clicking and caracoling and was accorded a short clatter of applause.

"The Danse Macabre," said Cicely to her companion; "one of Saint-Saens' best known pieces."

"Is it?" said Larry indifferently; "I'll take your word for it. 'Fraid I don't know much about music."

"You dear boy, that's just what I like in you," said Cicely; "you're such a delicious young barbarian."

"Am I?" said Larry. "I dare say. I suppose you know."

Larry's father had been a brilliantly clever man who had married a brilliantly handsome woman; the Fates had not had the least intention that Larry should take after both parents.

"The fashion of having one's lunch in the open air has quite caught on this season," said Cicely; "one sees everybody here on a fine day. There is Lady Bailquist over there. She used to be Lady Shalem you know, before her husband got the earldom—to be more correct, before she got it for him. I suppose she is all agog to see the great review."

It was in fact precisely the absorbing topic of the forthcoming Boy-Scout march-past that was engaging the Countess of Bailquist's earnest attention at the moment.

"It is going to be an historical occasion," she was saying to Sir Leonard Pitherby (whose services to literature had up to the present received only a half-measure of recognition); "if it miscarries it will be a serious set-back for the fait accompli. If it is a success it will be the biggest step forward in the path of reconciliation between the two races that has yet been taken. It will mean that the younger generation is on our side—not all, of course, but some, that is all we can expect at present, and that will be enough to work on."

"Supposing the Scouts hang back and don't turn up in any numbers," said Sir Leonard anxiously.

"That of course is the danger," said Lady Bailquist quietly; "probably two-thirds of the available strength will hold back, but a third or even a sixth would be enough; it would redeem the parade from the calamity of fiasco, and it would be a nucleus to work on for the future. That is what we want, a good start, a preliminary rally. It is the first step that counts, that is why today's event is of such importance."

"Of course, of course, the first step on the road," assented Sir Leonard.

"I can assure you," continued Lady Bailquist, "that nothing has been left undone to rally the Scouts to the new order of things. Special privileges have been showered on them, alone among all the cadet corps they have been allowed to retain their organisation, a decoration of merit has been instituted for them, a large hostelry and gymnasium has been provided for them in Westminster, His Majesty's youngest son is to be their Scoutmaster-in-Chief, a great athletic meeting is to be held for them each year, with valuable prizes, three or four hundred of them are to be taken every summer, free of charge, for a holiday in the Bavarian Highlands and the Baltic Seaboard; besides this the parent of every scout who obtains the medal for efficiency is to be exempted from part of the new war taxation that the people are finding so burdensome."

"One certainly cannot say that they have not had attractions held out to them," said Sir Leonard.

"It is a special effort," said Lady Bailquist; "it is worth making an effort for. They are going to be the Janissaries of the Empire; the younger generation knocking at the doors of progress, and thrusting back the bars and bolts of old racial prejudices. I tell you, Sir Leonard, it will be an historic moment when the first corps of those little khaki-clad boys swings through the gates of the Park."

"When do they come?" asked the baronet, catching something of his companion's zeal.

"The first detachment is due to arrive at three," said Lady Bailquist, referring to a small time-table of the afternoon's proceedings; "three, punctually, and the others will follow in rapid succession. The Emperor and Suite will arrive at two-fifty and take up their positions at the saluting base—over there, where the big flag-staff has been set up. The boys will come in by Hyde Park Corner, the Marble Arch, and the Albert Gate, according to their districts, and form in one big column over there, where the little flags are pegged out. Then the young Prince will inspect them and lead them past His Majesty."

"Who will be with the Imperial party?" asked Sir Leonard.

"Oh, it is to be an important affair; everything will be done to emphasise the significance of the occasion," said Lady Bailquist, again consulting her programme. "The King of Wurtemberg, and two of the Bavarian royal Princes, an Abyssinian Envoy who is over here—he will lend a touch of picturesque barbarism to the scene—the general commanding the London district and a whole lot of other military bigwigs, and the Austrian, Italian and Roumanian military attaches."

She reeled off the imposing list of notables with an air of quiet satisfaction. Sir Leonard made mental notes of personages to whom he might send presentation copies of his new work "Frederick-William, the Great Elector, a Popular Biography," as a souvenir of today's auspicious event.

"It is nearly a quarter to three now," he said; "let us get a good position before the crowd gets thicker."

"Come along to my car, it is just opposite to the saluting base," said her ladyship; "I have a police pass that will let us through. We'll ask Mrs. Yeovil and her young friend to join us."

Larry excused himself from joining the party; he had a barbarian's reluctance to assisting at an Imperial triumph.

"I think I'll push off to the swimming-bath," he said to Cicely; "see you again about tea-time."

Cicely walked with Lady Bailquist and the literary baronet towards the crowd of spectators, which was steadily growing in dimensions. A newsboy ran in front of them displaying a poster with the intelligence "Essex wickets fall rapidly"—a semblance of county cricket still survived under the new order of things. Near the saluting base some thirty or forty motorcars were drawn up in line, and Cicely and her companions exchanged greetings with many of the occupants.

"A lovely day for the review, isn't it?" cried the Grafin von Tolb, breaking off her conversation with Herr Rebinok, the little Pomeranian banker, who was sitting by her side. "Why haven't you brought young Mr. Meadowfield? Such a nice boy. I wanted him to come and sit in my carriage and talk to me."

"He doesn't talk you know," said Cicely; "he's only brilliant to look at."

"Well, I could have looked at him," said the Grafin.

"There'll be thousands of other boys to look at presently," said Cicely, laughing at the old woman's frankness.

"Do you think there will be thousands?" asked the Grafin, with an anxious lowering of the voice; "really, thousands? Hundreds, perhaps; there is some uncertainty. Every one is not sanguine."

"Hundreds, anyway," said Cicely.

The Grafin turned to the little banker and spoke to him rapidly and earnestly in German.

"It is most important that we should consolidate our position in this country; we must coax the younger generation over by degrees, we must disarm their hostility. We cannot afford to be always on the watch in this quarter; it is a source of weakness, and we cannot afford to be weak. This Slav upheaval in south-eastern Europe is becoming a serious menace. Have you seen today's telegrams from Agram? They are bad reading. There is no computing the extent of this movement."

"It is directed against us," said the banker.

"Agreed," said the Grafin; "it is in the nature of things that it must be against us. Let us have no illusions. Within the next ten years, sooner perhaps, we shall be faced with a crisis which will be only a beginning. We shall need all our strength; that is why we cannot afford to be weak over here. Today is an important day; I confess I am anxious."

"Hark! The kettledrums!" exclaimed the commanding voice of Lady Bailquist. "His Majesty is coming. Quick, bundle into the car."

The crowd behind the police-kept lines surged expectantly into closer formation; spectators hurried up from side-walks and stood craning their necks above the shoulders of earlier arrivals.

Through the archway at Hyde Park Corner came a resplendent cavalcade, with a swirl of colour and rhythmic movement and a crash of exultant music; life-guards with gleaming helmets, a detachment of Wurtemberg lancers with a flutter of black and yellow pennons, a rich medley of staff uniforms, a prancing array of princely horsemen, the Imperial Standard, and the King of Prussia, Great Britain, and Ireland, Emperor of the West. It was the most imposing display that Londoners had seen since the catastrophe.

Slowly, grandly, with thunder of music and beat of hoofs, the procession passed through the crowd, across the sward towards the saluting base, slowly the eagle standard, charged with the leopards, lion and harp of the conquered kingdoms, rose mast-high on the flag-staff and fluttered in the breeze, slowly and with military precision the troops and suite took up their position round the central figure of the great pageant. Trumpets and kettledrums suddenly ceased their music, and in a moment there rose in their stead an eager buzz of comment from the nearest spectators.

"How well the young Prince looks in his scout uniform" . . . "The King of Wurtemberg is a much younger man than I thought he was" . . . "Is that a Prussian or Bavarian uniform, there on the right, the man on a black horse?" . . . "Neither, it's Austrian, the Austrian military attache" . . . "That is von Stoppel talking to His Majesty; he organised the Boy Scouts in Germany, you know" . . . "His Majesty is looking very pleased." "He has reason to look pleased; this is a great event in the history of the two countries. It marks a new epoch" . . . "Oh, do you see the Abyssinian Envoy? What a picturesque figure he makes. How well he sits his horse" . . . "That is the Grand Duke of Baden's nephew, talking to the King of Wurtemberg now."

On the buzz and chatter of the spectators fell suddenly three sound strokes, distant, measured, sinister; the clang of a clock striking three.

"Three o'clock and not a boy scout within sight or hearing!" exclaimed the loud ringing voice of Joan Mardle; "one can usually hear their drums and trumpets a couple of miles away."

"There is the traffic to get through," said Sir Leonard Pitherby in an equally high-pitched voice; "and of course," he added vaguely, "it takes some time to get the various units together. One must give them a few minutes' grace."

Lady Bailquist said nothing, but her restless watchful eyes were turned first to Hyde Park Corner and then in the direction of the Marble Arch, back again to Hyde Park Corner. Only the dark lines of the waiting crowd met her view, with the yellow newspaper placards flitting in and out, announcing to an indifferent public the fate of Essex wickets. As far as her searching eyes could travel the green stretch of tree and sward remained unbroken, save by casual loiterers. No small brown columns appeared, no drum beat came throbbing up from the distance. The little flags pegged out to mark the positions of the awaited scout-corps fluttered in meaningless isolation on the empty parade ground.

His Majesty was talking unconcernedly with one of his officers, the foreign attaches looked steadily between their chargers' ears, as though nothing in particular was hanging in the balance, the Abyssinian Envoy displayed an untroubled serenity which was probably genuine. Elsewhere among the Suite was a perceptible fidget, the more obvious because it was elaborately cloaked. Among the privileged onlookers drawn up near the saluting point the fidgeting was more unrestrained.

"Six minutes past three, and not a sign of them!" exclaimed Joan Mardle, with the explosive articulation of one who cannot any longer hold back a truth.

"Hark!" said some one; "I hear trumpets!"

There was an instant concentration of listening, a straining of eyes.

It was only the toot of a passing motorcar. Even Sir Leonard Pitherby, with the eye of faith, could not locate as much as a cloud of dust on the Park horizon.

And now another sound was heard, a sound difficult to define, without beginning, without dimension; the growing murmur of a crowd waking to a slowly dawning sensation.

"I wish the band would strike up an air," said the Grafin von Tolb fretfully; "it is stupid waiting here in silence."

Joan fingered her watch, but she made no further remark; she realised that no amount of malicious comment could be so dramatically effective now as the slow slipping away of the intolerable seconds.

The murmur from the crowd grew in volume. Some satirical wit started whistling an imitation of an advancing fife and drum band; others took it up and the air resounded with the shrill music of a phantom army on the march. The mock throbbing of drum and squealing of fife rose and fell above the packed masses of spectators, but no answering echo came from beyond the distant trees. Like mushrooms in the night a muster of uniformed police and plain clothes detectives sprang into evidence on all sides; whatever happened there must be no disloyal demonstration. The whistlers and mockers were pointedly invited to keep silence, and one or two addresses were taken. Under the trees, well at the back of the crowd, a young man stood watching the long stretch of road along which the Scouts should come. Something had drawn him there, against his will, to witness the Imperial Triumph, to watch the writing of yet another chapter in the history of his country's submission to an accepted fact. And now a dull flush crept into his grey face; a look that was partly new-born hope and resurrected pride, partly remorse and shame, burned in his eyes. Shame, the choking, searing shame of self-reproach that cannot be reasoned away, was dominant in his heart. He had laid down his arms—there were others who had never hoisted the flag of surrender. He had given up the fight and joined the ranks of the hopelessly subservient; in thousands of English homes throughout the land there were young hearts that had not forgotten, had not compounded, would not yield.

The younger generation had barred the door.

And in the pleasant May sunshine the Eagle standard floated and flapped, the black and yellow pennons shifted restlessly, Emperor and Princes, Generals and guards, sat stiffly in their saddles, and waited.

And waited. . .

A Note About the Author

Saki (1870–1916) was the pen name of British novelist and short story writer Hector Hugh Munro. Born in British Burma, Munro was the son of Inspector General Charles Augustus Munro of the Indian Imperial Police and his wife Mary Frances Mercer. Following his mother's death from a tragic accident in 1872, Munro was sent to live in England with his paternal grandmother. In 1893, he returned to Burma to work for the Indian Imperial Police but was forced to resign in just over a year due to serious illness. He moved to London in 1896 to pursue a career as a writer. He found some success as a journalist and soon published *The Rise of the Russian Empire* (1900), a work of history. Emboldened, he began writing stories and novels, earning praise for *Reginald* (1904), a short story collection, and *When William Came* (1913), an invasion novel. Known for his keen wit and satirical outlook on Edwardian life, Munro was considered a master literary craftsman in his time. A gay man, he was forced to conceal his sexual identity in order to avoid criminal prosecution. At 43 years of age, he enlisted in the British cavalry and went to France to fight in the Great War. He was killed by a German sniper at the Battle of the Ancre.

A Note from the Publisher

Spanning many genres, from non-fiction essays to literature classics to children's books and lyric poetry, Mint Edition books showcase the master works of our time in a modern new package. The text is freshly typeset, is clean and easy to read, and features a new note about the author in each volume. Many books also include exclusive new introductory material. Every book boasts a striking new cover, which makes it as appropriate for collecting as it is for gift giving. Mint Edition books are only printed when a reader orders them, so natural resources are not wasted. We're proud that our books are never manufactured in excess and exist only in the exact quantity they need to be read and enjoyed.

bookfinity™

Discover more of your favorite classics with Bookfinity™.

- Track your reading with custom book lists.
- Get great book recommendations for your personalized Reader Type.
- Add reviews for your favorite books.
- AND MUCH MORE!

Visit **bookfinity.com** and take the fun Reader Type quiz to get started.

Enjoy our classic and modern companion pairings!

Classic & Modern